OVER YOU

By

H.M. WARD
&
L.G. CASTILLO

LAREE BAILEY PRESS
www.HMWard.com

COPYRIGHT

LAREE BAILEY PRESS
First Edition: February 2016
ISBN: 9781630351014

OVER YOU

CHAPTER 1

I sprint down the hospital corridor, dodging patients, other visitors and a delivery guy with an enormous bouquet of flowers. My heart is pounding so hard I'm afraid it'll crack my ribs. There's not enough air, and the stitch in my side brings tears to my eyes, but I don't stop—I can't.

The overhead fluorescent lighting casts an eerie glow on the sterile decor, and the sound of the bulbs makes my tired eyes twitch. I focus on the sound of my footsteps, rhythmic and reliable. He'll be okay. Things won't end here today.

Seven hours ago, I was in Texas, about to eat dinner. My only worry was studying for the graduate school admissions test I planned to take next semester. But that was before my sisters called to let me know they were rushing our father to New York City's Mt. Sinai Hospital. They didn't say much, only that I needed to travel as fast as possible.

When I walked away from New York, it seemed like a good idea. I wanted my own life, my own space, and two thousand miles in the middle made it impossible for my mother to meddle. I didn't expect this. I never thought my dad could slip from this world before I returned home.

Turning the corner, I see an information desk and a friendly looking nurse. She's a little older than me—late twenties, early thirties at the latest—with bright violet eyes and a stethoscope slung casually around her neck.

"Excuse me," I pant, "can you please point me in the direction of room 651? I'm David Bennet's daughter, Beth."

She reaches up and squeezes my hand reassuringly. "It's down the hall to the left and around the corner. You're a good daughter flying up here so fast."

"Thanks," I say, grateful for her kindness. I take off down the hall at a quick clip. I increase my speed when I'm away from the nurse's station and round the corner without slowing. I see the tall man in the dark suit just seconds too late.

We collide and I bounce backward. I tilt dangerously, preparing myself for an ungraceful landing, but he reaches out for my elbow and pulls me to his chest, steadying me.

His bright blue eyes gaze down intently into mine and—just for a moment—I forget why I'm here. Those eyes hold a lifetime of pain and a wealth of secrets. For a split second, the depths of his torment are reflected in those twin blue pools, and I sense a kindred spirit in him, like he understands my fear of loss all too well.

He blinks, clears his throat, and sticks his hands abruptly in his suit pockets, letting me fall away from his chest and out of his spell. "Darcy. William Darcy."

"Beth," I say my name instinctively, as a warning bell goes off silently in my mind. "Elizabeth Bennet."

He looks around nervously as if he'd rather be anywhere else right now, but he doesn't leave. He runs his hand through his dark hair and then glances at me again.

Darcy. Why does that name sound familiar? Wait a minute!

"William Darcy of Darcy Biopharm?" I take a step forward, poking his surprisingly muscular chest right in the middle of his expensive designer tie. I'm normally not so aggressive, but this man is a shit, I know that for certain. "What are you doing here? Putting my father in the hospital wasn't enough? Did you come to pull the plug, too? Or just kick him while he's down?"

Darcy blinks and takes a step back. "I had little to do with it. Maybe you should ask your father what he's been hiding."

"Don't insinuate you know my father better than I do." I glare up into his face and narrow my gaze to thin slits. My fingers twitch at my sides, wanting to ball up into fists so I can clobber this monster.

William Darcy has a strong reputation for being a heartless dick. He destroys without remorse, completely calloused from the inside out. His calm exterior irritates me. "Miss Bennet, I suggest you—"

"What? Take advice from you? No, thank you." I push past him without giving myself a chance to feel guilty for my manners. Fuck him. I wish I could say it to his face. As I start to rush away, I round and walk backward for a moment. "And don't show your face here again. You're not welcome."

"It's a free country, Miss Bennet."

"Kiss my ass, Mr. Darcy."

CHAPTER 2

"Beth, thank God you're here," my older sister, Jane, cries as I enter the hospital room. Her blue eyes look as tired as I feel. She rushes across the room, throwing her arms around me in a hug. "The doctor is just about to tell us if Dad can go home."

"I still don't see what all the fuss is about," Dad says in a weak voice from the hospital bed.

"You passed out at your meeting with William Darcy. It's a damn good reason to fuss since he hates you and the feeling is mutual," my baby sister, Mary, says from her perch in the window. She looks like a raven in a tree, her dark, Goth-style clothing contrasting vividly with the stark white window facing. "I imagine he prefers people consciously listening while he talks."

"Manners, Mary," Jane echoes mother, but more sweetly. Mary rolls her eyes.

"Technicalities," Dad says lightly. "Sit with me, Beth. I'm happy to see you, but you shouldn't have flown all the way here on my account." He shoots a sideways glance at Mary, who shrugs in response.

"She was long overdue for a visit. If she doesn't fly home every six months or so, she'll be wearing cowboy clothes and talking with a twang. Nobody wants that, raht, Beth?" Mary smirks, trying not to laugh as she does her worst Texas accent impression.

No one in my family understood why I chose to go to school so far away. It was a necessary evil. I needed to figure out who I am and how I fit into this world. I couldn't do it with certain people present. Okay, not people.

My mother.

She's like gravity—you can't escape her downward pull unless you leave for outer space. Texas might as well be outer space to my family of pedigreed New Yorkers. I like it, though. People are always nice, going out of their way to help a stranger, and no one hurries anywhere for any reason. If you walk slowly on a city sidewalk in New York, you get shoved to the pavement and trampled. Nothing moves slowly here. The city is always breathing, beating, pulsing like a rave, with no end in sight. In comparison, Texas is quaint and charming, a respite from the energy of the life the rest of my family lives.

I sit down on the bed next to Dad and take his hand. It feels lighter than usual, and his skin is yellow and paper-thin. All of him is paper-thin—when did he change so much?

Dad licks his dry lips and glances at me disapprovingly. "Stop looking at me like that, Elizabeth, it's just a virus. The doctor is going to get me some elephant antibiotics, and I'll be as good as new in no time."

Before I can respond, the door opens, and my mother breezes in with a doctor in tow.

She's speaking in overdrive, running her words together. "Now, of course, he'll be going home tonight! Don't be silly, Dr. Wade, a man heals best at home in his own bed." The doctor opens his mouth to speak, but she talks over him. "Dear me, no, we won't hear any more about it. Imagine! Expecting us to sleep here? Overnight? No one could get any proper beauty sleep in a place like this—the noise, the sheets, the sick people! No, Dr. Wade, you'll write us the necessary prescriptions, and we'll be on our way." Her gaze lifts, and she notices me. "Elizabeth, how nice to see you."

Translation: How could you run out on your family!

She smiles tightly and tips her head to the side.

Translation: I'll deal with you later, and you won't like it.

I skip the pleasantries, which also irritates my mother. "Mom," I begin, "if the doctor thinks Dad should—"

"Nonsense," she interrupts in a tone that means there will be no discussion. "David will be happier at home, won't you, dear?"

Dad nods silently from the bed, suddenly mute. I hate it when he does that! He just sits back and allows Mother to steamroll him. He openly adores Mother, but she's much less affectionate toward him. Their relationship is so one-sided. I sometimes wonder how they got married at all.

Dr. Wade finally finds a moment of silence large enough to voice his concern. "Mr. Bennet, I strongly suggest you consider staying here this evening for observation. It's only one night. I know it's not the Ritz, but I'm sure you understand." His eyes bounce from my mother to my father, as if deciding what to do, then he begins scribbling furiously on Dad's chart.

What the hell is going on here? There's more to this story, a lot more.

"Girls, would you give us a moment, please?" Mother gestures to the hallway with one hand.

"Mom, let us stay." I'm not ready to act like nothing is wrong. That's all we ever do—smile, nod, and talk about the weather. I'm sick of it.

Mother shoots me an icy glare. "No slang, Elizabeth. Call me Mother or nothing at all. I asked nicely, and won't repeat myself a second time." She clasps her hands tightly on the rail of Dad's bed, narrowing her gaze dangerously at me.

"Come on, Beth. Mom doesn't want us here." Mary takes my hand as she walks by, tugging me away from Dad.

Reluctantly, we shuffle into the corridor, the door shutting resolutely at our backs and muffling everything said behind it.

"What's going on? Why didn't you tell me Dad was sick?" My eyes flash accusingly from Mary to Jane.

"We didn't want to distract you from school." Jane blushes and looks at the floor before continuing. "Dad insisted nothing was wrong. He was going to work, attending meetings, and gone for most of the day. He seemed more stressed than usual, even a little run down, but we thought he just needed more sleep. He hasn't had seizures until today, and we texted you the instant he was on his way to the hospital."

"Beth," Mary says, her eyes staring straight into mine, "we don't know any more than you do right now. I promise. I'd tell you everything. Mother is, well, Mother." She rolls her eyes. "And you know how Daddy is. He takes pride in being able to care for us. This experience must be weird for him."

I sigh and lean back against the wall, sliding down until I hit the floor. Mary and Jane join me, all of us staring blankly at the gray wall across the hallway. One minute turns to two, two minutes turn to five.

Mary rests her head on my shoulder. "I've missed you."

"Likewise, Little Lamb." Old nicknames stick, even after years apart.

Mary smiles, and I see a moment of peace on Jane's face. She may be my older sister and have her shit together in front of everyone else, but in front of me, there are no walls. She tells me everything. The truth is, Jane struggles with such a massive amount of pressure she's usually doped up on Xanax to cope with it.

She's the eldest daughter, the most talented of the three of us, and swiftly passing prime age for a first marriage. The thought makes me want to puke. Who plans a first marriage with the expectation there should be a slew of others after that?

Not me.

I want love, marriage, and forever. One man, one love, one life, and a shoe full of kids. Needless to say, the odds of my becoming a spinster increase daily. Prince Charming must be trapped in a tower, somewhere, unable to get free and waiting for rescue. Maybe a dragon ate him, and I'll never find him. I'm not even certain what I'm looking for, just that I don't want to settle for the first eligible bachelor my mother suggests.

Jane, on the other hand, is too sweet and obedient to stop Mother from meddling in her life, always ready to please anyone except herself. It makes her miserable, but she can't stop. It's who she is, and why she needs Mary and me. We're the defiant ones, acting as a buffer between Jane and mom.

Jane leans forward and wraps her thin arms around her ankles. I think she's lost weight. Her silky blonde hair falls forward, hiding her face. "Do you think he'll be all right? Mother wouldn't have kicked us out if he wasn't seriously sick."

"I don't know," my voice is soft, careful. "I haven't seen him look that frail, ever."

Mary clears her throat and kicks her feet out, so we are all staring at her shit-kicker boots. "Beth, you haven't visited for nearly a year. The change looks more sudden to you. We see him every day. I noticed him changing a little bit, but I thought he was getting older. I didn't see any more to it."

"And Mother acts like nothing is going on," Jane adds softly.

"Maybe she doesn't know?" I ask.

Mary snorts and looks me in the eye. "When has our mother not known everything? No, she's fully aware of the situation and doing what she can to play defense."

"It feels more like keep away." Jane has tears in her eyes. "It's not fair. Dad is a good man—he shouldn't have to suffer like this!"

"What do you mean?" Mary leans forward and stares at her. "Dad's not suffering. What are you talking about?"

Jane has a natural ability to sense the emotions of another human being without trying. It's nearly impossible for her to ignore her family, and insanely difficult to hide things from her. "He is. Something's wrong, but I didn't think it was physical pain. I thought it was stress, but now I'm not certain. It's hard to tell. I'm sorry, Beth, I should have called you sooner. I thought…" She sighs, and I know what she's thinking. She doesn't trust herself anymore, not since Xanax dulled her senses. She walks around in a trance most of the time.

"Fuck it, I'm not going back to school this semester. I'm staying here. We'll figure out what's up with Dad, and, Jane, I love you, but we need to get you off the meds. They're screwing with you."

Jane ignores my last comment. She sits up and drops her knees to the floor. "You can't quit school!"

"I'm not." I shove in the two words before they freak out on me.

Mary blanches. "What about Mother?"

"I'll deal with her. I'm not quitting. I'm about to graduate. I can finish the few credits I need online from here and study for the grad school entrance exam. I don't have to be in Texas right now."

"I'd love for you to stay, but are you sure?" Jane looks at me with those big pale blue eyes, and I want to hug her until her head pops off.

I smile. "I've already decided. Now, all we have to do is find out what's wrong with Dad and play nice with Mother."

Mary snorts. "Is that all?"

We sit silently, staring at the wall again for a few minutes, none of us speaking—none of us daring to wonder out loud if Dad will still be with us in a few months.

CHAPTER 3

"Elizabeth, may I have a word with you?" Mother's been increasingly cold since we left the hospital. By the time we walk through the door of my parents' Manhattan apartment, she's an iceberg.

We've just finished settling Dad into bed, and she's standing at the entrance to his study, a tiny bookcase-lined room converted from a walk-in closet. There's barely space for the desk and chairs crammed in the middle. To disguise the lack of windows in this room, Mother installed floor-to-ceiling draperies perpetually closed across one wall as if there were windows behind them to hide.

I duck into the study and bite my lower lip. Mother is the main reason I left. We don't get along well. She wants to conform to society, and I want to defy it. Societal conventions are an absurd set of rules we pointlessly hold ourselves to for no other reason than because everyone else is doing it too. It's why sweet people like Jane pop pills to keep up with the breakneck schedules of other rich people in the city.

I'd rather tell them to go to hell.

Actually, I did that already, right before I left for Texas.

Mother plasters a stiff smile on her face. She closes the door and walks past me to turn on the desk lamp. It's sitting on top of a Bvlgari blotter made of hand-tooled leather. When did she get that? It had to cost over a thousand bucks. I don't understand why Dad lets her spend money this way. It nearly ruined us once already.

"Mother, I wish you'd told me Dad was sick." There I said it. Plain, direct and honest, but it doesn't make this moment feel any less childish.

Mother slides into Dad's massive leather armchair and gestures for me to sit next to her on the other. She sighs deeply, then looks into my eyes and matches my direct tone. "I tell you what you need to know, and you didn't need to know about this. Your job is school, and that's where you'll go back to first thing tomorrow."

"No, I'm not." My voice is stern, but my throat is too tight. "I'm staying here this semester."

She laughs once, harshly. "Oh, no, you most certainly are not. I've not paid in excess of fifty thousand dollars for your degree for you to throw it away months before graduation. You are returning to college, finishing your degree, and then moving back home. This is not open for discussion." Her words are clipped, and I know she's tired. I feel bad for her, how alone she must feel with Daddy sick.

I stand, and I know I shouldn't say another word, but they fall out of me like raindrops—a trickle at first, then a downpour. "I understand. When I left for Texas, I didn't mean to burn bridges with you, Mother. I simply needed space. If I'm still welcome in this apartment, I would like to take my final classes from here. I want to come home."

It kills me to admit it, but that's the crux of the matter—I want to come home. If she won't let me live here, I can't. I can't afford New York unless she helps me, and maybe some daughters are always welcome and can do no wrong, but I wounded her pride and rejected her way of life when I left. Things have been strained between us since.

Mother looks over at me slowly, considering me, her gaze scanning my jeans and t-shirt, the sloppy ponytail of brown curls tumbling off the back of my head. "You're not capable of conforming, Elizabeth. I will not endanger the status of this family for you to ease your conscience."

"Mother, I can. I'll do whatever you want. Just let me stay," I plead, tears prickling the backs of my eyes. "I miss my family."

Mother sits up, beaming. Damn it! I walked right into that—and it was what she was pushing for the whole time. Uhhggg! How did I not see it? She presses her palms to her lap and starts gushing details about the social season. "And of course, I expect you to attend every event to restore my faith in you, starting with the charity gala tomorrow evening. Your appearance, your manners, and your education will all be tested. Don't make me ashamed to call you my daughter, and you may stay as long as you like."

I nod. "Yes, Mother." I need a kick-me sign on my back because I'm the biggest dumbass there ever was. I fought to escape this living hell only to beg to be taken back.

CHAPTER 4

The grand ballroom hums with excitement. Men in tuxedos and women in an array of beautiful gowns mingle and whisper to one another. Diamonds twinkle from the ears, necks, and wrists of every woman in the room—except for the Bennet women, of course. I'm certain these other women didn't rent their dresses either.

Tables clad with crisp linens and adorned with extravagant vases of roses and gardenias circle an expansive dance floor. On stage, a full orchestra playing a waltz attracts a few older couples to dance with a certain grace that comes from age, years of marriage, and just the right amount of imported champagne. Wait staff weave through the crowd in sharp red jackets and pristine white gloves, dispensing flutes of champagne and hors d'oeuvres. The mood of the room seems to correlate directly with the weight of the champagne-laden trays—it lightens as they do.

"The Livingston family's financial holdings are doing well this year," Mother whispers, motioning to a table of rotund men and women all resembling sparkly penguins. I think Mother was a gossip columnist in another life. Maybe she's reliving her glory days. "At the table nearest them is the Sinclair family. My, my, if only their son weren't involved in the Diamond Reserve scandal," her eyes shine with genuine disappointment, "he would've been perfect for you Beth."

I imagine myself melting into the carpet or being hit by a flaming toilet seat—anything to avoid dwelling on the financial status of every family in the room.

I reach out desperately as a tray of champagne passes just outside my reach. Jane giggles at the look on my face. No champagne for me.

"Oh! There are the Ferros," Mother exclaims with shocked pleasure, enjoying private satisfaction at their expense. I steal a glance at their matriarch, Constance, and shudder. That woman gives me the creeps. She'd kill her own mother if it meant securing more power or money for her family.

My mother continues to tell us her thoughts, rarely stopping for air. "I didn't expect Constance to dare show her face with all the scandal surrounding her son Sean. Our Mary is a saint compared to him." Mother claps her hands gleefully and moves along, snagging a flute of champagne from a passing waiter's tray while motioning us to follow behind her.

It was the last flute on the tray.

"Look, there's Dad," Jane says with relief, directing our attention to the far right of the ballroom. We spot him standing next to John Rivas, a business client, and wave them over.

Never show them you're sick or you'll end up with a hostile company takeover. This room is filled with affluent men who miraculously bounce back, all smiles. Heart attacks, strokes, even cancer can't hold them down—nothing can. Which makes me wonder what's ailing Daddy. I still have no idea. I keep studying him for clues, but I haven't come up with any possible diagnosis yet. I'm hoping if I'm around more, Dad will confide in me. It's a long shot, but he might.

"I see you got here in one piece," Dad calls to us, stretching out his arms to hug me hello. Though he smiles brightly, his face still appears tired, and his once-substantial body is drowning in the fabric of his tuxedo.

"Hello, Daddy," I say, returning his hug, but trying not to squeeze him too tightly. "Good evening, Mr. Rivas." I turn to face Mr. Rivas, and he takes my hand, squeezing it warmly in greeting.

"Ah, Beth, Jane, you both look stunning. And Victoria, if David hadn't grown my profits twenty percent last quarter, I'd steal you away from him in a heartbeat." His dark eyes dance merrily as he reaches for Mother's hand and kisses the back of it.

"Dear me," Mother says, batting her lashes coyly. "You are a charmer. You must join us for brunch on Sunday. And bring your lovely wife. Is she here tonight?"

"I'm afraid not," Mr. Rivas says, his cheeks flushing slightly pink. "The last I heard, she was sunbathing on the Riviera. I'm afraid we lost touch after our divorce."

"Oh, divorce. What a pity." Mother beams, shifting her gaze to look at me encouragingly.

I can see the wheels turning in her head. Mr. Rivas is near Dad's age, and I can't say his name without instinctively adding 'Mister' in front of it. Bad match, Mom! Don't do it. Don't say it.

"Well, you know Beth here is doing very well for herself. She graduates college in a few months. Maybe you have a job for her, close to your office so you can personally show her the ins and outs of the business. That would be a wonderful opportunity, wouldn't it Beth?"

Shoot me. Someone. Anyone.

I glance around the room, desperate to escape Mother. Where's Mary when you need her?

"Doesn't that sound lovely, dear?" Mother addresses Daddy, who smiles blandly from behind his glass of champagne.

I smile until my face hurts. We're way past *Super Awkward Street* and quickly approaching *I Don't Give a Fuck Boulevard*, but I can't speed off that way. Mother made it clear that I need to follow her rules tonight.

I giggle and nod. "It sounds lovely."

Dad's bland smile crumples, and he stares at me as if I'd grown antlers. "Are you all right, Beth?"

I never giggle. I don't know where that came from. I nod too much and appeal to God for them to all look at someone else.

At that moment, I see a striking young man with bronze hair enter the ballroom. His face dances with excitement as he takes in the controlled chaos of the event.

"David, Charles Bingley is here." Mother immediately pivots to Jane and gives her the once-over.

Jane turns a light shade of green and shoots an apologetic look to Mr. Rivas, as Mother begins to pick imaginary lint from Jane's dress. A waiter with a full tray of champagne finally comes close enough for me to snatch two flutes.

"You don't have to do this," I whisper, handing Jane one flute of champagne. "Be strong. Say, no!"

"Bingley of Bingley Tech?" Dad asks. "Isn't he the man you wanted to meet, dear?" My parents continue their conversation unaware of the silent argument I'm having with Jane right under their noses.

"Of course, he's the one, David." Mother snatches the flute from Jane, and gracelessly tosses it back at me. "Don't be foolish, Jane. You can't mix alcohol with your medication."

I manage to catch it without spilling a drop and take a sip from both flutes. Knowing my mother is reason enough to double-fist champagne, but attending a gala with her practically requires it. Poor Jane.

"Victoria, allow me to introduce you to Mr. Bingley. I've known his family for years," Mr. Rivas says kindly. Introductions are part of this social circle. Walking up to someone you don't know and being all friendly is frowned upon. You have to be properly introduced. It's like a different era with these people.

Mr. Rivas, adds, "Look, he's brought Gwen and William Darcy with him."

The room is a rustling wave of colorful ball gowns swishing toward and swarming around the billionaire. Through the crowd, I catch a glimpse of a petite, willowy woman standing next to a muscular, broad-shouldered asshole in a tux.

"Oh, my," Mother gasps. "Mr. Darcy is even more handsome in person. Of course, no one is as handsome as you, David," she adds, just a beat too late.

I take another sip of my champagne, wishing I could chug it. "Is that William Darcy of Darcy Biopharm?" I pretend I don't know who he is— even though I'm shooting holes through him with my laser eyes.

"Yes, and the attractive woman next to him is his sister, Gwen." Rivas lowers his voice to a conspiratorial whisper. "Mr. Darcy keeps his sister on a short leash. Apparently, she's prone to making scenes at social functions, especially when she..." Rivas trails off, gesturing to my champagne. I immediately start looking for a place to dump my second flute. "Darcy guards his company's image jealously."

"Don't we all." I say it sweetly, wishing I could draw attention to the fact that corporations are not people, no matter what the law says. People should come first, but that's not the way this world works. Everything is done at the expense of the family to further the company, to build a dynasty. People are disposable, and family members are no different.

Those who don't make their own rules get removed from the game, like me.

Technically, I stopped playing and left. It's not the same.

I study the radiant Gwen and her brooding brother as I slip quietly back to ditch the second champagne glass on a nearby table. Darcy stands behind his sister, one hand resting on her arm like he owns her. By the way the women around him are acting, though, they apparently wouldn't mind becoming William Darcy's possession.

A voluptuous redhead wearing four-inch heels sashays past him. Being way too obvious, the woman brushes her well-endowed chest against Darcy's arm as she trips over an invisible object. Darcy visibly takes a step back, allowing Mr. Bingley to play hero instead. He's an ass, but that was well played. The woman flares her nostrils and stomps off, barely uttering a stiff thank you to Mr. Bingley.

There might be another reason why I dislike Darcy—he's arrogant about his greed. His reputation exceeds him, and while I don't know everything, I know enough. Family should come first, always. That's why I'm here. Treating Gwen like a pawn isn't all right with me, and just gives me another reason to push pins into his voodoo doll.

Mr. Rivas motions for us to follow and sets off across the room. Seeing no other alternative, I dutifully follow my family closer to the jackass. Dad heads straight for Darcy, whispering something to him that I can't quite make out.

Darcy nods once and they shake hands.

Mr. Rivas holds out a hand to Mr. Bingley, who clasps it warmly in both of his.

"John Rivas! It's a pleasure to see you, and you've brought friends, I see."

"Cameron, Miss Darcy, Mr. Darcy, allow me to introduce you to the Bennets." Bingley nods politely as Mr. Rivas makes the introductions, but his green eyes remain fixed on Jane. Mother vibrates like an excited Chihuahua.

"Cameron Bingley," he says, extending his hand and shooting Jane a dimpled smile. His eyes are kind and sincere. I like him instantly.

As introductions begin with the Darcys, Mr. Bingley remains transfixed by Jane.

"Please call me Gwen," Darcy's sister says warmly, seizing the opportunity to shake my hand and spur the conversation. Gwen is possibly more stunning up close, her long dark lashes framing magnetic blue eyes. "You can call my brother Willie," Gwen giggles as I turn to shake Darcy's hand.

"Very humorous, Gwen. I prefer the use of my surname if you must address me," he says sternly, his deep voice booming with irritation—as Gwen obviously intended for it to do. Even Darcy winces at the sound, but unapologetically holds out a hand in greeting nonetheless.

I don't want to slip my palm against his. There's a strange feeling spilling over me, pulling me toward him. He's attractive, yes, but his ethics and attitude are undesirable. They should cancel out any attraction to him, but I swear to God, my body is so high-strung that if we touch, I'll melt on the spot.

But it's too late. His hand is there, lingering, waiting for mine. If I don't shake it, all hell breaks loose, and if I do touch him—

"It's nice to make your acquaintance, William," I say, emphasizing his first name before beaming at him. I intend to slip my hand into his for a blink and withdraw. It's a hit and run handshake, but that's not possible.

On contact, a rush of electricity flows up my arm and swirls in my stomach. My mouth goes dry, and there aren't any words. I'm not convinced I'm still breathing. It's too hot in here. The way his thumb moves tenderly over my hand is almost erotic. The gentle caress makes my heart pound harder until the urge to snatch my hand from his is overwhelming. I slowly lift my gaze to meet his blazing sapphire eyes, prepared for recognition to set in.

But the awkward moment never comes. Is he just pretending not to recognize me?

Darcy's lips part as if he's going to say something, but no words come out. He just watches me from under those dark lashes. My eyes flick between his mouth and his eyes. I want him to speak, to say something, to tell me he remembers me, but he doesn't.

He just stands there, a full head taller than me, staring into my eyes with those perfectly pink lips parted. Suddenly I want to feel those lips on mine and his strong hands on my face, sweeping over my skin in a gentle kiss.

The thought shocks me. I'm not usually like this and I sure as hell don't swoon over assholes. What's wrong with me? Before I can figure it out, Darcy's sister starts laughing. She touches my shoulder, reminding me to drop Darcy's hand.

"Really, William," Gwen chides, laughing. "And you wonder why Cameron is your only friend? Don't mind my brother, Beth, dear. He abhors social settings and is only truly happy building his empire from behind his computer. Please excuse me." She bounces down the steps toward the center of the ballroom, calling out to another guest. "Jax, is that you? I haven't seen you in ages!"

Darcy takes in a breath as if to call after her, worry flickering in his eyes as Gwen disappears from his sight. He obviously cares deeply for his sister. His eyes flick back to me, a series of unreadable emotions crossing them before he breaks eye contact and pulls out his cell phone. Whatever tenderness he showed vanishes and the stern condescension reappears on that beautiful face.

And, I still want to kiss him.

I growl frustratedly in the back of my throat and walk toward Dad as the orchestra lulls to a stop, preparing for a new piece. Dad's cell phone buzzes loudly in the silence. He checks the screen apologetically, then turns to kiss Mother's cheek.

"Please excuse me, darling, I must take this call. Mr. Bingley, it was nice to finally meet you. Darcy, it was a pleasure to see you again. We'll have to arrange another meeting soon—I promise I'll be conscious at this one!" I frown as the men laugh politely at Dad's self-deprecating joke. Dad turns toward Mr. Rivas. "John, would you join me on this call?" Together, they disappear into the crowd.

The orchestra begins another waltz, and Cameron shoots a winning smile at Jane.

"This is one of my favorites," he says, gallantly holding out his arm to her. "Will you do me the honor?"

Jane blushes a delicate pink from the tips of her ears, to the neckline of her dress. She almost imperceptibly nods and accepts Cameron's hand, allowing him to lead her to the dance floor.

It's hard to believe someone as beautiful as Jane doesn't date more. I once read that beauty is intimidating, and most guys are probably too afraid to ask her out. Jane being too shy to initiate conversation with men doesn't help the situation.

I scan the room for the nearest table to hole up and hide, but am interrupted by a sharp elbow in my back. I turn to see Mother's eyes darting between Mr. Darcy and me, silently ordering me to encourage him to dance. My stomach rolls.

I study Mr. Darcy staring at his cell phone, oblivious to the silent battle of wills going on in front of him.

I look back at Mother and shake my head, "No."

Mother's lips form a thin line.

I shake my head harder.

Mother's eyes bulge in their sockets as a single brow lifts higher and higher.

I fold my arms across my chest and refuse to move.

A vein at Mother's temple pops up.

I estimate two remaining seconds in which I can ask Darcy to dance, or mother will do it for me. Shit.

I suck in a breath and slowly make my way over to the man. As far as I can tell, he doesn't see me. I'm standing there for a moment and finally manage, "Mr. Darcy?"

He doesn't look up.

I continue, "Would you like to—"

"No," he interrupts before I can finish speaking. "I have pressing matters to attend to right now." He rounds, and I watch his beautiful body in that tailored tux recede from sight.

I stand rooted to my spot, gaping after him in shock.

A second later Mother is next to me. She takes my arm and whispers, "Don't frown, dear. You'll give yourself wrinkles."

"Thanks, Ma."

She cringes at the informality, but doesn't comment on it. She pats my arm. "Never mind, Beth. I'm certain John has taken a liking to you. I'll make sure he attends brunch with us. I have the perfect outfit for you. It will bring out the color in your—"

Mother's face pales and her glass slips from her hand. I reach out for it, but it's too late. It hits the floor and shatters. That's not like her at all. People stare at us, trying to figure out why she's utterly still.

I stand back up and follow Mother's gaze. Holy crap!

Mary is marching into the ballroom, with guests discreetly gawking in disbelief as she passes. The high slit of Mary's black gown reveals shapely thighs covered by fishnet stockings and black shit-kicker boots. Purple fingernails peak from the freshly cut tips of her opera gloves.

I bite my tongue, suppressing a grin. In Mary's defense, she did exactly as mother asked her to do. She wore the dress, the gloves, fixed her makeup, and "did something" with her hair. Instead of the original two purple streaks, all of Mary's hair is now purple. It complements the studded dog collar she's wearing as a choker.

"Oh, Lord, I'm going to faint." Mother grabs my arm. I lead Mother to a nearby table, where she flops dramatically into a chair. "Beth, go after your sister. I can't believe it. I just can't believe she'd do this to me."

I run to catch up with Mary as she heads straight for Catherine Degatto and a crowd of her good ol' boy Texas billionaire business associates. They flank her three deep on each side, all clad in cowboy hats, boots, and tuxedos.

Although Mrs. Degatto is in her fifties, her face is flawless. She wears her silver hair in a short, sleek bob, with long side-swept bangs across her forehead. Mrs. Degatto tosses her head back and lets out that throaty laugh of hers, gray eyes sparkling with amusement in the conversation. For a moment, she is the stereotypical socialite, all manners and bluster and facade, but people who know her well know better than to get on her bad side. Her persona changes with her heartbeat, turning the poised and polished socialite into an ambitious powerhouse with eyes like ice and a spine of steel.

I try chasing after Mary discreetly, wobbling as I leap-run across the ballroom in my high heels.

"Mary," I whisper-shout. "Mary!"

Mary is only a couple of steps away from Degatto when she starts ranting.

"North Texas has experienced a record number of earthquakes since Degatto Industries and Frey Oil—hey!"

"Not now, Mary. Come on." I wrestle Mary away from the Texans before they hogtie her. "I admire your intentions," I whisper close to her ear, "but this is neither the time nor the place. Think of Dad." I steer her across the ballroom, toward the nearest exit.

"The people have the right to know," Mary complains as we reach the foyer.

"Mary, the people here know already and don't care. 'The People' to which you refer, do not attend Galas in $5000 dresses—shit-kicker boots or otherwise. Those people are at home drinking their poisoned water." I put a hand on her arm and wait for her to meet my eyes. "On an unrelated note, you have black lipstick stains on your teeth."

Mary sighs into the mirror. "Dad still thinks of me as the baby, you know, patting me on the head

~33~

like caring what happens to the world is a phase I'll outgrow. And while you're away finding yourself, I'm stuck here dealing with Mother."

It's like a sucker punch to the gut.

She's right, though, to escape Mother's crazy antics I'd chosen a university as far from her as I thought possible to attend—regardless of the cost to my sisters.

"Well, I'm back now, and we'll fix this together. We need to figure out what's wrong with Dad, first, though. Then we can tackle global warming, animal testing, and decontaminating the wa..."

I trail off at the sound of William Darcy's voice and drag Mary behind a nearby pillar.

"Hey! What's—"

"Shh."

"Is that William Darcy and Cameron Bingley?" Mary places a hand on my shoulder trying to get a look.

"Be quiet," I say with a scowl, waving my hand to shush her. "They're coming this way.

"William, a host of pretty girls are here, all dying to dance with you. I hate to see you standing off by yourself in a corner, acting like a mafia hit man. You could at least attempt to be sociable," Cameron says jovially.

"You know I hate dancing with women I don't know." His stoic nature is a defense mechanism. I sense it, wishing I knew more about him.

"Only because the moment you touch them, they swoon and fall in love with you." Cameron presses an arm against his forehead and bats his eyes. In a soprano voice, he squeals, "Oh, Mr. Darcy, your dancing is divine."

"Knock it off," Darcy answers with a smile that takes my breath away. I swear, my heart responds against my wishes, beating faster in response. My eyes drink in his thick, wavy hair, the stubbled shadow along his strong jaw, and the way his tuxedo strains across muscles too sinfully sexy for a pencil pusher. "Women don't talk like that," Darcy chuckles.

"Ah, but I'm not too far off."

"Perhaps. No one here is of interest to me. You've already attracted the prettiest girl in the room." His reply shocks me. I didn't realize he was aware Jane existed—or anyone else in the room for that matter. He's barely looked anyone in the eye since he arrived.

"Isn't she? Jane's the most beautiful woman I've ever met," Cameron breathes. "What about her sister, Beth? Jane speaks very highly of her. She's cute."

I wince.

"Some might call her cute," Darcy says as if he's just sucked a lemon, "if you like that nerdish girl look. She's not attractive enough to compensate for that smart-ass mouth of hers, though. Why are you out here anyway, Bingley? You should go back into the ballroom and enjoy your time with Jane instead of wasting your time with me. I'll find a way to entertain myself."

"What a fartknocker!" Mary cracks her knuckles and steps around the pillar, following them. "I bet I can knock that pussy out with one punch."

"No, Mary," I hiss. "Just walk away."

Mary can tell his comment felt like a fist to the face, so she nods and disappears into the crowd. They're just words, but to hear someone actually say they don't like you—that you're not beautiful—it cuts deeply.

I wander out of the ballroom and grab another flute, downing all of the amber liquid before I reach the balcony. The night air is warm for this time of year. Central Park stretches out below us, neat, green, and perfect. I walk over to the railing and lean on it, staring down at the grassy fields.

I'm lost in thought when someone shoves through the door and swears. He makes a beeline for the balcony and stops with a jerk when he sees he's not alone. The light from the hallway casts a soft glow on his face. Pain, shock, and surprise all mingle together and dance behind those blue eyes.

I look away, intending to walk past him and go back inside. "The balcony is all yours."

He doesn't reply. Instead, Darcy nods and swallows hard. His jaw locks and his fingers alternately stretch and still by his sides. No phone.

As I pass, his fingers brush against mine. The response is immediate, and the hollow of my chest feels full. I suck in a startled breath and stop. It's like I'm caught in a trap.

WALK, BETH! MOVE YOUR FEET! My mind screams at me to haul ass, but I can't move—not while his skin is touching mine.

Then it happens. That gentle touch turns to something more. Darcy clutches my hand and pulls me to him. He entwines his fingers with mine and lifts them between us. He slowly lowers his head and presses his mouth to my fingers, kissing them gently. The heat from his lips makes me shudder, and lightness fills my head, forcing me to breathe heavier.

Darcy says nothing, nor does he explain. He presses his forehead to mine and closes his eyes for a moment. When he lifts his lashes, our eyes lock. He blinks slowly, lowering his gaze to my lips. Pressed between our bodies, his fingers are so close to my skin I imagine their touch on more than just my hand.

We stay like that, suspended beneath the stars in a near kiss. It feels like hours pass before either of us moves again. It's Darcy who pulls away. He steps back, hanging his head between his shoulders as if ashamed of his actions.

I don't know if it's a slight to me, or if there's something else going on. "William?"

"Good evening, Miss Bennet."

CHAPTER 5

I hate everyone. I need to leave. The fact that Darcy hasn't left the party makes this feel even more awkward. I find a spot to sit at an empty table in the back, and a moment later Mary plops down beside me.

"Looking a little flushed, there, Sis. Making out in the coat closet again?" Mary has a crazy straw in a champagne glass filled with milk. She slurps it and waggles her eyebrows at me.

"You know it," I say flatly. "Nothing floats my boat more than doing it in other people's coats."

Mary makes a face and elbows me. "Ewww! I checked my coat! Now I have to get it cleaned again. Beth!" She shoves me dramatically, and I grin. "You're such a skank."

We dissolve into a fit of giggles and don't notice the man walking up behind us. We jump—and Mary shrieks a slew of curses—as a voice speaks from behind us.

"What are you two hiding from?"

"Colin!" I yelp and jump out of my chair to wrap my arms around his neck. "You scared the crap out of me."

He returns my hug tightly. When we finally let go, I look him over. He's wearing a new Armani tux with a pair of vintage saddle shoes. His pale blue eyes sparkle with flecks of gold, and his light brown hair is slicked back, making him look older.

Colin is my Texas twin. We're buds.

Grinning, I ask him, "What're you doing here?"

He frowns. "I'm here to kiss Catherine Degatto's ass. She's funding my father's campaign for Senate." He looks like someone killed his puppy. Then he turns to Mary and beams. "I'm loving the hair, by the way!"

"Colin, if you weren't BFFs with Beth, I'd host a sit-in protest in front of your penthouse in Frey Towers." Mary playfully punches his shoulder. "When are you going to grow a pair and force your dad to stop poisoning the water?"

"Um, ouch?" Colin rubs his shoulder. "Both physically and metaphorically."

Colin Frey has been my best friend since before my father moved his company to New York and we both attended Lakewood Academy together back in

Texas. Colin is the sole heir to the Frey Oil fortune, and his father, Michael Frey, will publicly announce his decision to run for Senate any day now.

In the meantime, Mr. Frey seems intent on ignoring his son except to further his own political interests. Mary is, of course, convinced his business practices at Frey Oil ignore the environment in much the same way.

"All right, all right," I say, stopping further debate. "Can we make this a violence-free evening? I'm not in the mood for picketing tonight, Mary. Maybe we can have a brawl tomorrow?"

"Ugh," Mary says and rolls her eyes, "you're such a killjoy. I'm calling it a night."

"Going home?" I ask skeptically.

Mary arches an eyebrow and laughs at me.

"Sorry, I forgot I was talking to the life of the party. I'll make up something to tell Mother."

"I doubt she'll mind. She'll be relieved I'm not here embarrassing her. Later, dudes!"

"You're going to miss out on the epic ass-kissing," Colin calls out as Mary heads to the exit. In response, she blows him a kiss, snatches it from the air, and slaps it on her own ass.

"I think I'll be ok," she says with a wink, before ducking through the door and escaping. Colin turns and hands me his handkerchief.

"Here, take this."

"What's it for?"

"Haven't you ever seen a billionaire's son with a brown nose?"

"Eww, Colin. That's gross!"

He puts an arm around my shoulder and speaks with his best Texas twang, "Honey, you ain't seen nothin' yet!

———

My eyes sweep nervously around the ballroom as Colin bypasses the tables and leads me into the center of the dance floor. I keep my back ramrod straight, my head held high and haughty, while my stomach is flipping like an Olympic gymnast. It's been years since I've played the elegant socialite, and it's never been a role I enjoyed. Too much attention, too many discreet whispers, too much fake.

In the crowd of guests, I pick out Jane, blushing as she listens attentively to Mr. Bingley. Nearby, Mr. Darcy seems to be on his phone again. He taps the screen with such force I'm surprised it hasn't cracked.

Colin takes my hand and sweeps me into his arms. I can do this. I can relax. Or I could run.

"What's wrong?" Colin asks, concerned.

"People are staring." They are.

I imagine their conversations in my mother's voice. 'Look at that little Bennet girl! Imagine them showing their faces here, as if they could afford to donate to charity. Profits are down, down, down, and it shows in their rented ball gowns!'

I glance from guest to guest, my stomach churning, panic rising in my throat. Colin lifts a hand gently to my cheek and forces my gaze back to him.

"They are staring because you look gorgeous, and they're curious how long we'll dance before I start hitting them up for campaign money."

"Oh, Colin," I say with a half-laugh, "well, we better give them their money's worth."

He leads me through several waltzes, whispering a heaping helping of gossip about the couples we pass on the floor. By the time Colin starts a game of "Are They Real," I'm relaxed again and enjoying myself.

"Fake. Fake. Real. Fake. That one," Colin discreetly studies the cleavage of a broad-shouldered woman I swear I've seen on TV as a linebacker for the Giants, "I genuinely have no idea." We both giggle.

"How do you know all this?"

"Oh, I know," he says, pausing near the orchestra. "I'll be right back. The Degattos seem to have requested funeral music, but I'll shake things up."

As Colin talks to the conductor, a throaty laugh catches my attention, and I turn in its direction.

Catherine Degatto and her daughter, Anne, stand on the edge of the dance floor talking at William Darcy. I see Anne tucking a strand of sleek hair behind her ear and fluttering her lashes. Ugh! Did Anne take the same how-to-catch-a-billionaire class every other woman at the gala attended? Anne lightly touches Darcy's arm, tips her head back, and laughs that throaty laugh again. She leans forward, letting one breast brush his suit. He can have her. He's a colossal asshat. They deserve each other.

"O.M.G.," Colin whispers in my ear, making me jump. "It's Anne Degatto. Her mother tried to hook me up with Anne last year. My mother literally dragged me to the Degattos' beach house in Maui. Anne and her mother wearing bikinis..." He shudders. "I've never seen so much cellulite!"

"Colin!" I elbow him. The Degattos may be bitchy, but no woman deserves having their cellulite critiqued out loud.

"Well, it's true," Colin mutters, rubbing his ribs. "You know Anne is an arts and antiquities dealer, right?"

I nod.

"Did you know her mother is Anne's biggest customer, the only reason her business is solvent?" Colin pauses expectantly for that information to sink in. In fact, I didn't know that and wish I still didn't. Colin continues, "There are rumors Degatto Industries is in secret negotiations with Darcy Biopharm; Catherine Degatto thinks she can buy Anne a husband the way she bought her a business to run. You know they're desperate if she considered ME a catch worthy of her daughter."

"Anyone would be lucky to have you, Colin."

"Tell that to my father." His pale blue eyes grow sad for a moment, but light back up watching Darcy accept Anne's graceless advances. "Seems like Degatto has her eyes on someone new for Anne. Poor dude. He doesn't seem to mind, though."

My eyes narrow, noticing for the first time how attentive Darcy is with the Degattos. No cell phone in hand, no expression of disdain on his face as he speaks. It's annoying how damned attractive he is when his face relaxes.

When Anne rises on her toes and whispers in his ear, he gives just a hint of a smile. It lights up his face and shows off his gorgeous features.

As if hearing my thoughts, Darcy's sapphire eyes suddenly lift and lock with mine.

Shit!

I look away quickly, scrambling for anything else to be doing, and accidentally step on Colin's foot in the process.

"Son of a—" he grumbles.

"Sorry," I say with a wobbling step in the opposite direction. From the corner of my eye, I catch a glimpse of Darcy's lip twitching into a grin.

"Really, Beth. I can't take you anywhere." Colin chuckles and takes my hand to lift me up and guide me away.

I'm already scanning the room for exits when I'm distracted by a familiar melody coming from the orchestra. I look questioningly at Colin, who shoots me a mischievous grin.

"Colin, is this your idea of shaking things up?"

He grins. "Our performance in the Lakewood Academy talent show was the highlight of my high school career." He extends his arm, spinning me away from him and transforming my dress into a billowing blur of purple.

"If that was the highlight your high school career, I almost feel sorry for you."

"You still remember our moves?"

"We only practiced them ten thousand times. They're ingrained in my muscles. We would've won, too, if not for Cinnamon Taylor and her pole dancing routine." We both make a face.

"Her routine wasn't that great," Colin says with a smirk, "but her boobs popping out while she was hanging upside down might've sealed the judges decision. They were pretty nice boobs."

"You noticed that?"

"Everyone noticed that! I'm gay, not dead." Colin's preference for men over women is a closely guarded secret my sisters and I have kept for years.

"Here comes the opening beat." Colin spins me out and then pulls me back to his chest. He smiles down at me, and we're off.

"This is still my favorite song," he pants as the beat picks up. He starts to sing, "Bei Mir Bist Du Shein... Dude, it means that you're grand."

I can't help it. I start laughing instead of worrying so much about the other people in the room.

"And beautiful! And what's the last major hit that had any Yiddish? Plus it's a song about hotness, and you're hot—I'm hot."

"Yeah, it's a hot time in the old town tonight." He leads me into a spin and twirls me out, lifts my hands up and then slides them down my sides.

What the? "Uh Colin, dear – that's not swing dancing."

"I know, but there are some hot guys here."

"Don't make me lead. You know I'll do it."

Colin smirks and the head tilt he offers suggests I couldn't lead even if I wanted.

My jaw drops into an O, and I stare at him with big cartoonish eyes for a moment. "Yeah, you're done, pretty boy. My turn." I tug his wrist and pull-push him into submission.

He frowns and balks slightly when I pull him close. He whispers into my ear, "That was low. You emasculated me in front of my friends." He's grinning. I can feel it.

I tease back, "Don't be silly, you don't have any friends. Now, can we finish this little dance with a bang?"

"We better, everyone is watching."

I blanch as I look around. Crap, they are watching—even Darcy who is looking extra judgmental with Anne at his side. He walked away from me. And he's an ass.

"Done, and if you feel like you can do the throw, go for it."

Colin seems surprised. "Really? You sure?"

"Yup. Go for it."

Colin takes the lead again, spins me out, and we fall into the routine, William Darcy completely forgotten. I feel confident, sexy, and not the least bit klutzy, as we move across the dance floor. Other guests move back and form a circle, watching us dance. Briefly, I catch sight of Jane, Cameron Bingley still beside her, both clapping and cheering for us. I lock my eyes on Colin's, anticipating his moves and following where he puts me. The guests around us become one big blur until nothing remains but the music.

It's been a long time since I've danced like this, and my breathing sounds more like panting. Colin spins me again, sending my hair flying into my face, and I toss it back, laughing. Colin chuckles too, and I notice he's also breathing heavy with the effort of the routine.

Then, with a dimpled smile, he pulls me to him and slides his hand along my cheek. He dips me back and says, "Kiss me." He sings the words, perfectly on pitch, and watches me. He knows I won't kiss people I don't love, but I do love him.

I pull on the back of his neck, and his lips come down on my mouth. It's a long, sweet, chaste kiss. A moment later, he swings me out again, and I giggle in a whirl of emotion.

I wonder what Darcy thought about that kiss. I wish I could look at him and see if he's still there, jealous or cold. Odds are he's still standing there with an icicle up his ass, but you never know.

The couples that were dancing have faded away. I'm no longer certain if they're there or not. Colin keeps my gaze fixed on his face as we come close before twirling me out.

"Let's do it," he says, breathlessly.

"Go for it." He spins me out and then back. People love seeing spins and the flutter of the hem of my dress. The only thing they love more are throws. Have I mentioned throws are hard? It requires complete trust, and I rarely offer any.

This is crazy.

It's been ten years.

This is insane.

I'm going to fall on my face. Insta-nose job. The hotel will probably sue me for ruining their floor.

The movement feels normal, like I've done it before, so when he grabs my waist, dips down low, and then swings me up high the first time, I'm all smiles. When I slam into his body, my legs V around his torso with my feet next to his head. I know what's coming next. There's enough adrenaline flowing through me to power LIPA.

I dip backward and reach for the floor, crawling between his legs while he swings a leg over my head. He jerks me upright, spins me around, and grabs my waist. This time, I'm going straight up, all the way upside down.

The song crescendos as my heart slams into my chest, exhilaration flooding my body in waves, and then he does it. I swing up, our arms lock, and I kick my feet over my head for a beat before he swings me down so that my legs wrap around his waist. He spins us in a circle, laughing, and kisses my face—grinning so widely I know he's truly happy in that moment.

Colin's life is such a mess it's rare to see him like this. I kiss him back and hold up his arm, encouraging the crowd to clap for him, and they do.

He shifts me up higher to unlock my legs, then lowers me back to the ground. My arms and legs are shaking, and I fall into his face, smooshing him. It's totally graceless, but I don't cower or cry—this was too perfect.

"Mour fer lel."

I pull back and laugh. "I'm sorry. What'd you say?"

"I said yours are real."

"Colin!" I feel a blush set my cheeks on fire as I swat at my friend. He sets me down and beams at me.

"That was awesome," Cameron says from behind me. We turn to face him, and Colin drops his hand to my waist, loosely holding me. "Mr. and Mrs. Bennet, you have a very talented daughter."

Mother rushes over, no doubt horrified by my lack of conformity. I hope I don't have to live in a box because of this. She did suggest I dance with someone.

"That's very kind of you to say, Mr. Bingley. Though I wouldn't call that spectacle talent." Mother shoots an icy glare in my direction. "Now, Jane, on the other hand, is very talented."

Colin glances at me, letting Mother's comment roll off. The next song begins, and couples are dancing to slower swing this time. I feel Colin start to sway to the beat next to me.

"Mother," Jane murmurs, embarrassed. Poor kid.

Dad claps Colin's shoulder affectionately. "That was quite a finale."

"Really, Beth," Mother says. "That... That... Whatever that performance was should be left for professionals. Oh! Your gown!"

I look down to find the beautiful rented dress torn at the hem. Damn, I hope she insured it.

"I'll mend it when we get home," I say. Mother glares down her nose at me disapprovingly.

"Oh, Mr. Darcy," Mother says gesturing behind me, her voice dripping with desperation. "What did you think of Beth's dancing?"

He turns to me. He's so close, I can catch the scent of him. My stomach twists and I notice Colin holding me tighter. Damn it, he can tell what Darcy does to me.

Darcy carefully selects his words. "What you did out there was... something. Like nothing I've ever seen before."

I scowl.

Before I can respond, Mother steps between us, ending our stare down. "Mr. Bingley, Jane dances divinely, don't you think?"

Jane gasps, pink flooding her perfect face.

Cameron's green eyes glow as he looks at Jane.

"She most certainly does. It's like dancing with an angel."

"She's had lessons from the top dance instructor in the city. He came highly recommended from Catherine Degatto. Do you know Catherine, Mr. Darcy?"

"Of course. She's a trusted business associate." William emphasizes the word 'trusted,' but Mother babbles on without catching his insult.

Mother goes on to tell him how she and Degatto are close friends (they aren't) and how my father often gives Degatto financial advice (he doesn't).

I glance over at Dad to see what he thinks about Mother's little white lies, but he doesn't seem to be paying attention. After checking several different screens on his cell phone, he absentmindedly excuses himself to make another call. Mother doesn't even notice him leave.

"Dancing isn't the only talent Jane has, Cameron—may I call you Cameron?" She doesn't wait for him to answer. "She's also an outstanding artist. She painted the mural in the new wing of the children's hospital. It's magnificent. Even the mayor said he'd never seen such beautiful art. He's considering commissioning Jane to do some pieces for his Martha's Vineyard home, you know (he's not)."

At this comment, Darcy's eyes snap toward Mother disapprovingly. His head nods slightly, as if confirming something to himself.

"Really? I didn't know that," Cameron says with genuine interest. He runs his hand through his silky hair and offers a shy smile. "I don't know if you've heard, but I—"

"May I have a word with you," Darcy interrupts, his voice stern.

"Excuse me," Cameron smiles as Darcy pulls him aside.

Mother's jaw drops at the rude interruption.

I'm not surprised. Despite my dislike for the man, if I were in Darcy's situation, I'd want to protect my friend from being manipulated, too.

I watch Cameron frown at Darcy, shaking his head as if he can't believe what he's hearing. All of this is easily solved by people just minding their own business. It's obvious Cameron likes Jane. Darcy and Mother just need to let things sort themselves out.

"Jane, don't just stand there. Do something, anything," Mother hisses. "Mr. Bingley must invite you to his home."

"I-I-I don't know what to say," Jane stammers, her skin turning green.

"Well, figure it out before he returns."

Jane nods and looks like she may hurl on the spot. I hate this. I wish Mother wouldn't push her so hard, but I have no idea how to make things easier for her.

Just when we could all use a good distraction, Gwen runs up to Colin, her face shining.

"That was spectacular! Where did you learn to dance like that? Hi, I'm Gwen, by the way," she says to Colin, "William's sister."

At that moment, Darcy suddenly joins us again, as if we can't be trusted alone with his sister.

"Colin Frey," Colin says while shaking her hand.

"Oh, Colin Frey! I know your mother, Andrea," Cameron exclaims on Darcy's heels. He reaches out to shake Colin's hand as well. "I sit with her on the Children of the Military charity board. Sorry to interrupt. You were saying?"

"I was telling Gwen that Beth and I learned the moves from..." Colin glances sideways at me and grins. "A dance studio that uh, well—"

"We took lessons at Arthur Murray," I interrupt, rescuing Colin from his memories.

"You remember the Russian?" Colin asks me, his eyes glittering with mirth. Our instructor was a very friendly Russian, who preferred to instruct Colin how to move with his hands.

"Who could forget the guy? He was hot." I say the last word about two octaves higher than normal.

Colin leans in and whispers in my ear. When I glance up, everyone is talking—everyone except Darcy. He's staring straight at me, looking as though he wants to tear Colin apart.

I smile and don't look up again.

CHAPTER 6

A bright light hits my face, making me wince.

"BETH! Wake up!"

I groan, opening my eyes, disoriented. Jane is perched on the edge of my bed, shaking me awake.

I was dreaming about Darcy and that kiss. "I'm dreaming about him now? Wonderful!" I pull the pillow over my face, horrified, remembering the way he made me feel—the way I wanted him to make me feel. Disgust coils in my stomach like an angry snake.

Jane's panic recedes for a moment. "Wait, you had a dream? About who?"

"More like a nightmare," I mumble from under the pillow.

"What?"

"Nothing," I say peaking around the pillow at Jane, who looks radiant even at this ungodly hour "It's not important. What time is it?"

"7 a.m."

"Ugh, Jane, it's too early!" I roll over, pulling the pillow fully back over my head. The instant I leave the bedroom, Mother will nag nonstop about last night—about the party, about my shenanigans with Colin, about insulting William Darcy. Thank God she doesn't know I kissed him on the balcony.

I sigh, allowing the corners of my mouth to rise into a peaceful bliss. If I don't think about what a horrible man he is, that kiss could be a magical memory for cold, lonely nights. As is the jealous look Darcy shot our direction when I walked off with Colin last night. Secretly gay BFFs rock!

"Don't go back to sleep. I need you to tell me what to do. I got a text from Cameron," Jane says, biting her lip.

"Really?" I'm impressed. Apparently, whatever William Darcy told Cameron last night, Cameron chose to ignore it. "That's great Jane!"

She pushes a strand of blonde hair behind her ear. Her face scrunches up as she says the next part. "He wants to know if I'm available to paint the mural in his new cottage."

"No way!" She nods. "So, then why do you look so worried? You'll totally rock that mural."

"I don't think I should take the job."

"Why not?"

"While you were dancing with Colin, Mary texted me, warning me about William Darcy." Jane twists her hands nervously. "She told me what he said about you."

"Jane, William Darcy is a condescending shit, and you don't need to worry about him. I do wonder how someone as sweet as Cameron Bingley would consider someone like him a friend? Maybe Cameron's on some mission—you know, adopt an asshole, change a life."

Jane giggles.

"I don't care what Darcy thinks of me. Cameron is perfect for you, though, and I like him. I mean, what's not to like? He's attractive, considerate, and, most importantly, recognizes sensational dancing when he sees it." I wink at her, and Jane's face lights up.

"Are you sure you're okay with this?"

"Of course. You like him don't you?"

"Yes, I do," she says, her eyes dancing. "Do you genuinely think he likes me, Beth?"

"I watched him all evening, Jane. When he wasn't dancing with you, he still couldn't take his eyes off you. He wants you. He wants you bad!" I giggle as Jane smacks me in the face with a pillow before leaping from the bed.

"I have so much to do. I have to draw out my plans and gather my supplies." Jane suddenly pales at the thought of going alone. "If I panic, you'll help me won't you?"

"Of course! That's what sisters are for."

Jane bounces around the room grabbing clothes then hurries into the bathroom. I've never seen Jane so excited!

————

With Dad at work and Jane and Mother on their way to Mr. Bingley's cottage, the house is quiet. I pad into Mary's room with a mug of hot coffee warming my palms. She's face down, spread-eagle on the bed, her purple hair strewn over the pillow. She's still wearing her black bra, a lace hipkini, and her shit-kicker boots. Very pretty. And funny. Damn, Mary.

I give her a nudge. "Wake up, goober. I got you coffee."

She squirms and her angel wing tattoo peeks out from under the edge of her bra. Between the wings are the initials S.L.G, the initials of her best friend, Sofia Lynn Gonzales, who died of cancer a few years ago.

Though a high school student at the time, Sofia's death was national news. The Gonzales family lived in a trailer park near a field where Degatto Industries was drilling for natural gas. There were rumors the water was contaminated. Degatto Industries lawyers denied any wrongdoing on behalf of the company and convinced government officials that the sudden prevalence of cancer in the area was coincidental.

Mary hasn't been the same since Sofia's death.

Mary can be rash at times, but her end goal is justice for Sofia. Every cause Mary takes on helps those who can't fight back on their own—like Sofia's family. It's not a bad way to lash out and deal with loss, but I still worry about her.

I want her to find some peace before she implodes. If she can make a difference, even a little one, I think it'll help.

Mary groans, flipping to her back. Black lipstick is smeared all over her face and across her pillow. Dark smudges shadow the skin under her eyes, giving her already pale complexion a deathly aura. I shudder.

"We're the ninety-nine percent," she mumbles.

I chuckle. Even in her sleep, she's in activist mode. "Mary, wake up. I need your help."

"Ink, not mink," she breathes, hugging a pillow to her chest.

"Mother just got back from Kaufman's furs. You should see the coat she bought."

She jolts out of bed in a panic. "No way! She promised me she wouldn't do that. I can't believe that woman!"

"Wait, Mary. Wait!" I laugh, catching her before she sprints out of the room. "I'm kidding. She took

Jane shopping and then to Bingley's cottage. Here, have some coffee." I shove the steaming mug into her hands.

"It's too early for this. Remind me to beat you with a stick later."

"It's three o'clock in the afternoon."

"Oh," she takes a sip, making a face. "Man, my head's pounding. I shouldn't have taken on Colin's bet."

"You were with Colin?"

"Yeah, after the gala. I ran into him at that new club, Six Degrees. He was hooking up with some Latin hottie."

I'm impressed. Six Degrees is the newest and hottest club in the city—and almost impossible to get in.

"Colin has some serious dance moves." She takes another sip of coffee, waving her hand. "Oh, yeah, he told me about the show you two gave at the Gala. Man, I miss all the exciting stuff! Wish I could have seen Mother's face during your big finish." She snorts, "I bet you didn't think half of Manhattan's elite would ever see your ankles over your ears, huh, Beth?"

I elbow her as she snort-laughs while trying to sip her coffee. "Drink your coffee, buttface."

"Sticks and stones. So, what's up with Jane and Cameron? Did they hook up?"

"Yeah, in the coat closet." Mary's eyes go wide. "Do you believe everything you hear? Cameron just asked Jane to do the mural."

"And Mother made sure Jane looked her best." Mary rolls her eyes.

"Yep. There's no way Dad can afford Mother's spending. The dresses, even rented, cost a few thousand, plus shoes, and jewelry."

Mary nods from behind her cup, only coming up to add, "I have no clue where the family heirlooms went. Those disappeared a while ago."

"I noticed. Usually, Mother makes Jane wear them, but I haven't seen any of them, either. Even her old wedding rings are gone. She had on some huge rock I've never seen before. Mary, this has to stop. Dad won't slow down because Mom won't. I need to see how bad things are, but I can't do it alone."

She shrugs. "Sure, what do you need from me?"

"Help hack into Dad's computer?" I make a face, expecting her to say no. It's a horrible invasion of privacy, but I won't have him working to pay my bills anymore, not after this. And if I have to live in a box, I will. It's better to have him sick than not have him at all—and anyone can see he's not getting better, no matter how much he smiles.

Mary clasps her fingers together and stretches, popping her knuckles. "Like I'd say no. I'm on it, Beth!"

————

I wander into Dad's home office—also known as the closet—and flick on his desk light. I know he duplicates his files somewhere, and it'd be much harder to hack his work computer. I just hope Dad backs up his financial records on this machine, too.

After I turn on Dad's computer, Mary walks into the room free of her zebra stripes and munching on a bagel. As she sits, her bath towel slides from her head, allowing dark wet hair to spill over her shoulders.

"Seriously? The purple was a washout color?"

"Of course."

"Mother's going to freak when she sees you look normal."

"That's the point." She grins, placing fingers over the keyboard. "Let's see how long it takes me to hack into Dad's accounts."

She shakes her head, tsking softly to herself. "Why do old people use birthdates as passwords? Jeeze, this needs better protection!"

"Later, Mary. Pull up that file." I point to a spreadsheet marked 'P&L' in his tax folder.

Her fingers fly over the keyboard and within a few minutes, Excel files pop up onto the screen revealing the profit and loss statements for the last three quarters. Her brow furrows.

"This is worse than you thought. Have a look at this." She angles the computer's screen toward me.

My jaw drops. No wonder why Dad feels like crap. There's so much red I feel sick just looking at it.

A door slams and Mother's voice drifts down the hall. "Jane, don't be ridiculous. I just dropped you off a couple of hours ago, and you already want to come home?"

"Crap! Go!" I gesture for Mary to sneak out as I shut off the computer. I follow her into the hallway and nearly crash into her back. Mother is in the kitchen for the moment. Mary and I sneak into the living room just as Mother walks out, her hands filled with at least a dozen shopping bags and her cheek pinning her phone to her shoulder.

She drops her purse on a nearby gold-gilded antique marble table. "Get control of yourself, Jane. This job is the opportunity of your lifetime. Bingley Tech is currently in negotiations to merge with the largest software company in the world. Can you imagine how much money Cameron Bingley is worth?"

Mary makes a gagging sound as she plops onto the couch. Mother throws her a glare. When she eyes Mary's hair, her nostrils flare. "I'll deal with you later, young lady."

Mary rolls her eyes, tossing the last piece of bagel into her mouth.

"I won't hear any more of your whining, Jane. You will take the job, and you will stay there until it's complete. Now, be a good girl and take a Valium." With that, she clicks off the phone and tosses it to the side.

"Beth, I'm shocked by your behavior last night." Mother slips off her designer heels and leans back into the couch looking exhausted. Yeah, hours of spending Dad's hard-earned money will do that to you.

"I heard she and Colin rocked the ballroom last night," Mary says, grinning.

"The word 'rock' does not begin to describe their indecent behavior. No wonder Colin has no affection for you other than friendship." She stands and heads back to the kitchen as she continues speaking. "How could he take someone so unsophisticated seriously?"

"Um, maybe 'cause he's gay," Mary mumbles.

I shake my head at Mary. Mother doesn't know Colin is gay, and Colin swore my sisters and me to secrecy. It's never been an easy topic, but now that his father is running for Senate, it's a campaign-ending scandal waiting to happen. The thought makes me sick. Colin's a great guy and a loyal friend. He doesn't deserve the crapstorm that's going to fall on him.

In the other room, the sound of cabinet doors and shopping bags goes quiet. "What did you say?" Mother isn't in a good mood.

"I said, maybe we should pray," Mary calls out, winking at me.

"Young lady! This is no laughing matter." Mother strolls back into the room with a martini in hand. "Your sister not only managed to embarrass herself and Colin, but she also riled Mr. Darcy."

Yes, Mr. Darcy and his delicious kisses. He was very riled up.

Mother continues ranting. I'm not paying attention until Mary elbows me. She tips her head toward Mother. "She's going to kill you first, and I had purple hair and boots on last night."

"I know. I've always been lucky like that."

Mother glares at us. "Honestly, I'm surprised Mr. Bingley even called Jane. He must be a gentleman to overlook your behavior. Beth, must you turn every conversation into an argument?"

"Yes," I smile at her. "Mom, I didn't mean to, besides, Darcy has a stick up his butt—he hates everyone." My phone vibrates, and I glance down.

It's Jane. I pretend to listen to Mother as she continues her lecture about appropriate social behaviors. In between texting, I hear words like "charm school," "millionaire matchmaker," and "tattoo removal" coming from her high-pitched, nasally voice.

> JANE: *Help me!*
> ME: *What's wrong?*
> JANE: *I can't do this.*
> ME: *Sure you can. You're a great artist. Wow them, babe.*
> JANE: *It's too big. I can't take it all in.*

I suppress my urge to giggle, but Mary notices.

"What is it?" Mary snatches my phone. A broad grin spreads across her face. "You go, girl!"

"To whom are you speaking, Elizabeth?" My mother's voice hovers between annoyance and interest.

"Colin. He wants to marry me." I take back the phone before Mother sees the texts. She huffs at my silly diversion and focuses her attention back on Mary.

> JANE: *The room. It's huge.*

I chuckle and type a reply.

ME: *The mural you did at the children's hospital was big.*

JANE: *This room is 2x that size—and it's not just a room, it's a whole movie theater.*

ME: *Wow, really? A theater? I thought it was a cottage?*

JANE: *They keep insisting it is a cottage—one that houses a full-sized movie theater within it. The guest bathroom is bigger than our bedroom.*

ME: *That's great!*

JANE: *IDK. I think this is a bad idea. He said I could stay here since it'll take longer than I'd planned, but I can't. Beth...*

ME: *Want me to come over and help?*

JANE: *Really? *Happy dance**

ME: *Sure. I'll borrow Mary's motorcycle and be there in a couple of hours.*

JANE: *OMG. I owe you one!*

ME: *TTYL*

CHAPTER 7

I turn off the motorcycle, still feeling the rush as I sit for a moment in the circular driveway staring in disbelief. No wonder Jane is freaking out. Who calls a two-story mansion a cottage? Crazy-ass rich people. This place is huge.

I lock my helmet to the bike and attempt to smooth down my windblown hair while hitching up my backpack. I trudge up to the front door and ring the bell. The house is beautiful, made of limestone gleaming white in the summer sun. The roof is copper, and the patina is a pale green. It looks like a French chateau wedged in the middle of Long Island.

The front door is cast iron with decorative scrolling. A large copper lion's head holds a circle in his mouth, beckoning me to touch it. As I reach for the lion, the door swings open.

A young woman wearing a light gray uniform opens the door. Her hair is tied back into a tight bun, keeping her dark hair off her long face. Her high cheekbones and olive skin give her an exotic look.

"May I help you?" Black eyes narrow as they look me over. Although her words seem curious, her meaning is clear: Who the fuck are you?

"I'm Beth Bennet, Jane's sister."

The housekeeper's face suddenly breaks into a smile. "Ah, Miss Jane's sister. Please do come in. We're expecting you. I'm Bea, Mr. Cameron's housekeeper. If you need anything during your stay, please ask me. Mr. Cameron and his guests are at the pool. Please follow me."

Jane hasn't been here for more than a few hours and already Bingley's staff adores her. If Jane could only see how awesome she is, maybe she wouldn't have so many panic attacks.

Our footsteps echo in the foyer. I try not to gawk as we walk through Cameron's home. I keep my head pointed forward while my eyes take in the opulence surrounding us. I suck in a breath as we walk down a plastered Venetian hallway with coffered ceilings. My fingers itch to touch the panels, but I stick them into the pockets of my jeans. I can't afford to replace anything I break.

We come to a grand staircase that winds down to a lower level. Hung directly in the center of the room is an enormous chandelier. At the top of the landing, I can see outside into the gardens. Everything is green and lush, with large trees set further back to allow sunlight to flood the grounds just outside the doors below.

As we descend the stairs and near a pair of arched French doors, I can hear laughter and splashing.

The back of Cameron's house is even more magnificent than the front. When I step outside, I'm awestruck by the sweeping lawn. There are acres of perfectly cut grass and gardens filled with a rainbow of flowers. Impossibly, it's prettier than I expected.

The terrace is incredible, featuring a cascading Italian fountain flanked by four small fire pits. And the pool! Eight ornate fountains line its length, sending a steady stream into an expanse of sapphire blue.

Gwen's slender body glides through the water doing the backstroke. Her white bikini highlights her tanned skin. "Hey, Beth!" She waves.

"Beth, you made it." Cameron walks up to me with a big grin on his handsome face. "You remember Gwen and William Darcy, of course, and have you met Anne Degatto?"

My eyes slide right past Anne to Darcy, who looks annoyingly gorgeous wearing nothing but a pair of swim trunks. His dark lashes fan against his high cheekbones as he stares, yet again, into the screen of his smart phone. His thick hair is wet and slicked back. Droplets of water fall from the curls at the nape of his neck onto his tanned, muscular body. I think I'm going crazy. I can't stop staring as the droplets slide across an incredibly broad shoulder and roll slowly between well-defined pecs. When my eyes reach his abs, I have the insane urge to lick the droplets from them.

Yep, I'm losing it. I press my hand against the helmet mark on my forehead. Maybe the helmet prevented my brain from getting oxygen or something. I need to avoid him, but here he is. Damn it.

Darcy glances up for half a second, and my reaction is instant. My stomach dips into my shoes, and I swear he lassoed me because something is pulling me toward him—to those perfect lips on that wicked body.

STOP IT!

I look away, huffing breaths like I've been running. He's a bad man, Beth! No hanky-panky with bad guys. You don't even like him. Stop it.

When did I become a hornball? This isn't like me, not at all.

As if hearing my thoughts, his sapphire eyes flick to mine. They widen a moment as they drift from my borrowed shit-kickers to the black jacket covered in dirt and a few bugs that committed suicide on the leather. His eyes snap back to mine, his handsome face a mask. He nods slightly then returns his attention to his phone.

Anne clears her throat, catching my attention.

"Yes. I know Anne. Hi," I say, trying to keep my eyes off Darcy.

Anne narrows her dark eyes and gives me a cool nod. She's wearing a dark bikini top that makes her skin look pasty—it's not flattering. She still has that constipated expression she wore last night.

She places a perfectly manicured hand possessively on the arm of Darcy's chair before returning to her book. My eyes bounce from her to William and realize she thinks I want him. Yeah, that isn't going to happen. On the contrary, I think she's perfect for him. The two of them were made for each other.

"Jane's in the theater. Maybe you can convince her to take a break and join us," Cameron says. "Come with me, I'll—"

"Mr. Cameron," the housekeeper approaches him with a phone in her hand. "It's Phil Cates returning your call about the merger."

"I'll show her where the theater is," Gwen says, climbing out of the pool. "I'll even give you a tour of the house."

"Yes. Please do. Thanks, Gwen." He looks at me apologetically before going back into the house. "Sorry, Beth. I have to take this."

After wrapping a towel around her perfect body, she pokes Darcy and says, "When I get back, that phone better not be in your hand, big brother, or I'll throw it in the pool. You're supposed to be on vacation!"

She pads over to me, whispering in my ear. "He needs a distraction big time. Anne's not helping at all. The moment she stepped outside wearing that awful bikini, William grabbed his phone. His eyes have been glued to it ever since."

I choke back a laugh.

"Some people work for a living," William says. "Unlike some who leech off others' hard-earned assets." His eyes briefly flick to me.

What the hell! He's referring to me. He had to be. I can feel the veins on the side of my neck throbbing. I can't believe the gall of that man. He doesn't know me.

Before I can give him a piece of my mind, Gwen huffs, "I work."

"I'd hardly consider your dabbling in literary porn work."

"Neither would I call it literary," Anne says, lowering her book.

Gwen puts her hands on her hips. "Have you even read my work, Anne? You look like you could use some porn."

"Well, I never!"

"And you won't if you don't loosen up," she snaps back.

I'm starting to like Gwen, despite her brother.

"Gwen." William gives her a stern look.

She ignores him. "Seriously, Anne. Just look for my books under my pen name, Debbie Dallas."

"You're Debbie Dallas? The Debbie Dallas of the Hot Texas Nights series?" Texas Nights is a wildly popular series currently selling like hotcakes. All my friends from college were talking about it. The lead male character, Jackson Travis, is totally my book boyfriend. "I love that series!"

"Ooh, a fan," Gwen says. "I knew there was something I liked about you."

"Why does that not surprise me?" William gives me a stern look.

"Knock it off, William. If you're such a gentleman, why don't you take Beth's luggage into the guest room where she and Jane are staying?"

He lets out a breath, his face looking annoyed, but he stands anyway. "Where is your luggage?"

"Here." I slip the backpack from my shoulders, throwing it to him. It smacks against his chest and falls to his feet. His lip twitches before I turn to Gwen and walk with her back into the house. "So tell me, Gwen, is the stripper carrying Jackson's baby or is she lying about him being the father?"

CHAPTER 8

On the way to the theater, Gwen plays tour guide through Cameron's richly decorated six-bedroom, seven-bathroom vacation home. Behind a hidden door located between the dining room and the front entryway, she reveals what she refers to as her favorite room in the entire house: the wine cellar. As she speaks knowledgeably about some of her favorite wines, I can't help but think of what John Rivas insinuated about her alcohol problem.

When we reach the library lined with imported Honduran mahogany bookshelves, I drool.

"This is amazing," I say, unable to stop my hands from stroking the silky smooth shelves.

"Aren't they?" Gwen replies. "Anne is not my favorite person, and I hate the way she throws herself at my brother, but she does have good taste. Cameron bought most of this home's artwork and furnishings from her."

"Cameron's a sweet guy."

"Too sweet. When Catherine Degatto heard about Cameron buying this place, she insisted he hire Anne to decorate it—on commission, of course."

"She did an excellent job."

"I guess." She shrugs as she directs me out of the room. "Cameron's way more of a mortal than this house implies. He'd be just as happy with a gaming chair and a milk crate to stow his controllers. He only wanted this place to escape the stress of living in the city, claiming the country air releases his creative juices. Here we are." She stops in front a pair of oversized antique red doors, resting both hands on burnished brass Art Deco handles.

"These doors are fabulous!"

"Yeah, Anne did one thing right by finding these. She pulled them and several other pieces in this room from the demolition site of a deteriorated movie theater in Brooklyn. Do you know the time?"

I pull out my cell phone and check the screen. "It's almost seven."

"Crap! I'm meeting my editor for dinner in the city and need to dress quickly. Jane is inside the theater working already. I'm sure Cameron will join you once he finishes his call."

"Go ahead. I'll be fine."

"By the way," she calls, already heading the opposite direction, "don't mind my brother. He's all bark." Her feet slap against the floor as she jogs down the hall. "I think he likes you."

Yeah, right. I pull open the door and step inside.

Fully inside the theater, I feel as if I've been transported back in time. My feet sink into the thick red carpet. I hesitate, lifting my boots and look under them, making sure I'm not tracking anything in that could ruin the pristine carpet. Certain it's safe, I begin to descend a winding staircase, openly gawking at the gold satin painted railing and gold-flecked stars on the ceiling and carpet.

I pause at the last step, staring up at the gorgeous crystal chandelier in the center of the landing. Then I see something that makes me jump with delight—a full concession stand.

"This is so cool!" The black marble counter is spotless, gleaming underneath pendant lights. On the counter are rows of penny candy jars filled to the brim with colorful jellybeans, gumdrops, and every hard candy I can imagine. Boxes of chocolates and licorice line the shelves below the counter. I'm in heaven!

I inhale, and the delicious scent of fresh-popped popcorn makes my mouth water. Off to the side is a vintage popcorn machine, its polished red and silver outsides gleaming in the dim light. I squeal like a little girl and grab a small bag filling it to the brim with warm, buttery kernels.

"Beth, is that you?" Jane's voice comes from a dark corner of the room.

"Yeah. I'm coming." I quickly follow the direction of her voice, munching on popcorn. "Did you see all the candy? Mary would flip if she—oh!"

I turn a corner and discover the viewing area. Five rows of red velvet upholstered chairs face a screen so huge it covers the entire wall. Matching floor-to-ceiling drapes pulled back with a thick gold cord frame the screen. The other three walls host blank sheetrock panels lit for display by track lighting—a vast blank canvas waiting for life.

"OMG! This room is huge." I look around the room in awe.

"Told you so." Paint supplies and wads of sketch paper litter the floor around her. "I'm so glad you're here."

"Don't worry, Jane. You can do this. What's your plan?" I mumble around a mouthful of popcorn.

"I don't know."

"You must have some idea."

"Well..."

Jane always doubted herself. Despite winning countless awards for her artwork, she lacks the necessary confidence in her talent to sell her skills.

Volunteering to work on the mural at the children's hospital for free gained her the opportunity to do something fun, but when the hospital board offered to pay her for her time on a job well done, she refused. Art isn't about money for Jane, so she doesn't know how to act when money is involved.

"Is it that one?" I point to the sketch paper in her hand. "Let me see."

She looks at me warily. "Don't laugh."

"When have I ever laughed at something you've designed?" Wiping my hands on my jeans, I reach for the paper. "Now, my stick figure drawings, that's comedy." I take the large, thin paper gently into my hands, careful not to smudge any of her work. "Oh, wow, Jane! This idea is perfect!"

Jane has an incredible imagination. She's sketched the entire theater with each panel making up a piece of the mural. On one panel, there's a colorful drawing of penny candy jars, an unmistakable curly-haired Shirley Temple using a chubby arm to retrieve some candy. On the second panel, two teenage girls wearing poodle skirts flirt with a young man behind an old-fashioned ticket booth.

"Sorry to keep you waiting," Cameron calls, jogging down the stairs two at a time. "Did Gwen give you the grand tour?"

"You have an incredible home, and this theater totally rocks," I gush.

"Thank you. I'm so glad you'll be able to stay as my guest. And, please, eat all the popcorn you want."

I blush as he eyes the bag in my hand.

"Seriously, I want you to make yourselves at home. Mi casa es su casa." His green eyes gaze longingly at Jane. A delicate pink flushes her cheeks, and she busies herself with the supplies.

Aw, he's totally crushing on her.

"So, have you made any progress, Jane?" His voice caresses her name.

"I, uh, I—" Her eyes dart to me, pleading for help.

"Actually, she has. Take a look at this."

He studies the drawing for a moment. Jane looks at him, biting her lower lip nervously. Then he breaks out into a smile, his dimples flashing. "It's like you're reading my mind. This is exactly what I've been looking for!"

"Really?" Jane's voice is breathless. "Are you sure?"

"Yes, I'm sure. Your proposal complements the nostalgia I've been trying to create with this theater. I love how each of the panels represents a different era. You're very talented, Jane."

Jane's face lights up. "I can start right away if you want. I have some questions about the last panel. There are so many directions I can go with that one."

I sit on one of the red theater seats watching Jane and Cameron go over the plans. Just as I'm about to relax, my phone vibrates.

MOM: *Are you there, yet?*
ME: *yes*
MOM: *Good. Tell me you have the Jane situation under control.*
ME: *Everything's fine, Mother. She doesn't need me at all.*
MOM: *Good. By the way, Catherine called. She said you were rude to Anne.*

What, are we in third grade? She tattled on me? I barely spoke to her at all!

ME: *I'm sure it was a misunderstanding.*
MOM: *I hope so. Keep me posted.*
ME: *K*
MOM: *Also, tell Jane to wear the coral Missoni sundress tomorrow. It brings out the—*

I click off my phone not bothering to read the rest. The way Cameron looks at Jane, she doesn't need a designer dress to hold his attention. Things would work out on their own if Mother would stop using Jane as billionaire bait. Anyone can see Cameron's a good match for Jane. He's sensible, easy going, and friendly to everyone he meets.

The only thing I can't figure out is how someone like Cameron became such good friends with someone like Darcy.

CHAPTER 9

After Jane finally passes out, I slip from my bed and pull a sweatshirt over my head, covering my pajamas. I've not been here long, but dinner wasn't my thing. Who hires a personal chef to cook three roasted Brussels sprouts in a light vinaigrette for dinner? No wonder rich people are grumpy—they're all hungry!

There's an endless supply of candy in the theater, but I need protein. I wonder if I can get away with a run to Wendy's. Screw it! I'm doing it. I need a Frosty. After tugging on my boots, I sneak down the hallway. It's eerily quiet, and I'm a little spooked that I'll get caught by a ghost—or, worse, Anne.

Why is she here, anyway? I'm getting the distinct impression that no one likes her very much. She must be here at Darcy's request.

Speaking of the bastard who can't keep his lips to himself, he's all but snubbed me since my foot crossed the threshold. I think he'd rather snuggle poison oak than sit by me—which made dinner weird. Anne and I flanked him. I'm trying to be a nice guest, but Anne makes my eye twitch. She pretty much kept her talons dug into Darcy's leg all night.

I reach the kitchen, padding around back to the delivery entrance. If a door is still open somewhere in the house, it'll be this one. The kitchen staff is always here.

Except for now.

Damn it! I walk into the expansive empty kitchen and glance around. The alarm pad by the back door is glowing red, indicating that it's armed.

"Bloody hell! That's it. I'm going to starve to death."

"Yes," a voice behind me says, startling me enough to make me jump, "one Brussels sprout at a time."

I whirl around, clutching my chest. "Darcy! You asshat, don't sneak up on me!"

His brow lifts, making him appear mildly amused. "Asshat?"

My heart is still pounding in my chest. I suck in a few jagged breaths. "Would you prefer I call you something else?"

"Yes," he says with a nod, "something else entirely."

I shake my head, already knowing where he's going with this. "Yeah, Darcy. I got it."

He stares at the side of my face until my stomach flutters out of my mouth and flies away. I glance over my shoulder at him, "What?"

"Nothing, it's just…" he clears his throat, reaches over my shoulder, and punches a few buttons on the keypad. The light on the panel turns green.

I turn and look up at him. "You know the code!" I laugh lightly, sounding a little crazy. "I owe you a burger! Come with me."

It's totally a whim. For some reason, I enjoy the sound of his voice, that deep monotone he uses to snap at me.

Darcy's eyes widen and his lips part. "You want me to follow you where?"

"You're not following me. I'm taking you. Come on." I grab his wrist and pull him outside. We walk back to the garage, and I hold out my hand. "Tah dah! Jump on, dude. There's a Wendy's about a mile from here."

The night air is crisp, making me feel alive. I smile and inhale deeply.

"You want me to ride on that?"

I grab my helmet and shove it into his hands. "I bet girls say that to you all the time," I say, giggling as I pull out the keys.

He's still gaping. "You're serious?"

I swing my leg over the side and straddle the bike, bringing it to life. It roars, thanks to the hugeass exhaust pipes Mary had custom added. Where she found a Harley Fat Boy, I'll never know. It was probably compensation from PETA for freeing a pack of rabbits.

I rev the engine and call out to Darcy. "Come on, it's not far."

"You're not properly dressed."

I make a face and look down at my bare legs. My PJ shorts stick out a few inches farther than the fitted hem of the sweatshirt. Mary's boots are icing. I shrug. "It's Wendy's, not the Met. I don't need an evening gown, do you?"

Darcy folds his arms over his chest and bumps the helmet against his stomach. Did I mention he's wearing a clingy black shirt that looks so soft, and a pair of ass-hugging jeans? His hair is messy like he was doing something naughty. Ick, Anne.

I start to drive away, thinking he's not coming, but he reaches out for me. "Wait."

I stop and look back at him. He pulls the helmet on and tightens the strap under his chin before throwing his leg over the back of the bike. His hands slip around my waist, and he holds on loosely.

"Don't drop us. It'll ruin my jeans." His voice is deadpan. He doesn't care at all that my skin will get ripped off should we fall, but heaven help us if we scuff his fancy jeans.

I laugh darkly. "No problem, Darcy. No one is going down tonight."

Double entendre.

Before he can speak, I rev the engine, and we take off. His grip increases as we fly down the highway. After a few turns, he leans with me and seems all right.

At Wendy's, I treat him to a Baconator while I eat nuggets and suck down a shake. He lifts a fry, offering it to me. "I've never had someone in pajamas buy me dinner."

I smirk and take the fry. "I'm sure. They're probably naked, right?"

Darcy is biting his burger when I say it, and nearly chokes. A pickle falls from his lips as he gasps for air and tries to stop laughing. "You really think so highly of me?"

"Asshat."

"Yes, I recall. The vernacular of today's youth is very colorful."

I roll my eyes, pick up a fry, and chuck it at his face. It hits him right between the eyes on the bridge of his nose. "Your placid condescension speaks volumes, but your snobbery isn't welcome in present company."

He wipes the grease off his face while I speak. When he puts the napkin down, he studies me. "Convention has its place. Your outright rejection of it, regardless of situation, makes me think your inexperience controls your life. Inept actions snowball into half-assed decisions that blow up in your face. Sound familiar?" He's so cocky, so utterly arrogant.

"Don't be a bastard, too, or I'll have to leave you here."

He deflates and when he lifts his gaze to mine, there's sincerity in his voice. "Why must you defy everyone and everything?"

I don't look at him. I'm about to smile and blow off his question, but his voice drops to a whisper. "There's a time to fight and a time to build alliances, Elizabeth."

Holy shit, he said my name! I drop my nugget. It plops in the ketchup, forgotten, and I stare at him. "With you, I suppose?"

He doesn't reply. Those blue eyes pin me in place, and I like it. Why? Why this guy? I haven't felt this attracted to anyone ever. Why does it have to be Darcy?

We finish our meals in silence. Darcy trails behind me as we walk back to the bike. It's off to the side of the restaurant, in the shadows, parked underneath a massive tree on the corner of the property. The canopy is so vast that it dapples the ground in patches of black shadow from the back of the lot all the way to the street.

Darcy stops behind me. I turn to see why and nearly fall over he's so close. "Why did you kiss me the other night?"

What? I make a face, and turn away. Yeah, I'm not answering that. Darcy grabs my elbow and gently turns me around until my back is to the bike. He releases me and stays close enough to touch, but he doesn't. He lowers his face, making us close enough to kiss, but he doesn't lean in the rest of the way. He lingers, breathing hard, and letting his scent fill my head.

I want to kiss him, but I shouldn't. He's not like me. He doesn't value anything I do—this is wrong.

"Tell me," he commands an answer, but I'm unwilling to give him the satisfaction.

Instead, I use my stupid youthful brain and press my lips to his. That's all it takes for the attraction between us to ignite. His hands are on my face, in my hair, pulling me closer and kissing me deeper. His tongue sweeps the seam of my mouth greedily, wanting more. Before I'm aware of what's happening, his hands reach down to cup my butt. My legs wrap around his waist, and in three steps we're by the tree. He presses my back against the trunk and dips his head to my neck.

I can't think. I'm lost in emotion, in feelings so intense this doesn't seem real. His mouth is hot as it moves down my throat and onto my shoulder. The sweatshirt I'm wearing seems too bulky, and I want it gone.

I dip my head back, allowing him better access as my nails find the skin of his back. I want to run them along his skin and feel his body move into mine. I want him with me, inside me.

"No. God, no," I gasp, not realizing I've spoken until Darcy's grip loosens, and he steps away. His hair is hanging in his face, hiding those brilliant blue eyes from me. He looks around as his spine stiffens. I watch him turn to ice in front of me, the moment of heated pleasure is gone.

"I'm sorry, Miss Bennet. Please forgive me." Without another word, Darcy turns on his heel and walks away.

CHAPTER 10

Several days pass, and I can't stop thinking about Darcy. The way he kissed me was so unlike him, so passionate and pure. The man taints everything he touches, how could he kiss like that? How could I let things get so carried away?

Thank God Darcy's natural expression is placid. Who'd ever dream he pinned me to a tree and sucked on my neck until I lost control the other night?

I did see him with a Frosty later, though. He brought them home for Gwen and Cameron. I pretended not to notice, but I did. The guys sucked down the drinks like they'd never had anything better. It was hilarious. Silly billionaires don't know what's good.

As the mural progresses—and Cameron continues to adore Jane's ideas—she becomes increasingly more relaxed. Cameron frequently visits the theater to see her progress, even helping with the work where he's able. It shocks me how effectively Cameron coaxes Jane from her shell. I've never seen her so animated with people outside our family.

He stands close to her, his lips by her ear, whispering. Jane smiles and blushes. I can tell she adores his attention and admiration.

"Wow, I can't believe how incredible these look," Gwen coos as she walks into the theater. "OMG, Jane!" Her endless tanned legs move gracefully underneath a turquoise sarong, and her dark hair is wet like she just stepped out of the pool.

"Jane's brilliant. Don't you think?" Cameron gives Jane a gentle smile.

"Beyond brilliant. The mural looks extraordinary," Gwen says, looking around in awe. "You have mad skills. William should hire you to do something for his penthouse in the city."

I snort. Darcy doesn't seem like the kind of guy to hire an artist so fresh from school.

As if reading my mind, Gwen says, "My brother can be excessively discerning at times."

I raise an eyebrow. "You think?"

"Okay," Gwen admits, "he's needlessly picky. But when he sees Jane's work, I'm sure he'll love it. He's by the pool. I'll get him."

"Oh. That's cool," I say, busying myself cleaning paintbrushes. "We'll be leaving in a few hours. I'm texting Mother to send us a car." I can't put Jane on the back of Mary's bike. She has enough anxiety without feeling like she's in a freefall down the Cross Island Expressway.

"You can't leave now, Jane." Cameron's face falls as he looks at Jane. "We need to celebrate. Stay and swim with us! I'll have the chef make us that salad you loved so much, and maybe some of that pink champagne Beth enjoyed the other night?"

"I don't know," Jane looks at me questioningly. "Thank you for the invitation, Cameron, but we didn't bring swimsuits."

"Don't be silly," Gwen butts in, waving a hand at us. "I packed dozens of swimsuits with the tags still on them. I'm sure we can find something you like."

Jane looks at me, her eyes hopeful. I feel torn between wanting to avoid Darcy and staying. It would've been a no-brainer if Gwen hadn't mentioned he was back. I'd love another chance to fangirl Gwen and weed out some spoilers from her next book. What finally convinces me to stay, though, is the heart-breaking expression on Jane's face.

"Ok. Why not? We can leave in the morning."

"Yay!" Gwen drags me to the stairs. "I have a red bikini I know you'll look gorgeous in." She sings the last few words like a deranged Muppet. I can't help it. I laugh.

———

Jane and I sit in Gwen's room sorting through suitcases of designer bikinis and cover up dresses. All of them still have tags. I make the mistake of actually reading one price and gag. Eight hundred dollars! The suit is like three postage stamps connected with string. How can this be eight hundred dollars?

"They're freebies from my modeling days," Gwen explains.

"I can definitely see you as a model," Jane says, smiling warmly at her. "You're beautiful! And the way you walk, it's like you're always on a runway."

Gwen lifts a white one-piece swimsuit with a halter-top and hands it to Jane. "You'll knock Cameron's eyeballs out with this one."

Jane's cheeks turn pink as she accepts the suit.

"I miss modeling." Gwen sounds melancholy. "I wish William would let me work in that way again."

It really is none of my business, but the words spill out of my mouth unchecked. "Let you? What do you mean 'let you'?"

"Please don't misunderstand, William is only looking out for me. Our parents died when I was a baby, and he was seven. Friends of our family, the Wickhams, took us in and helped manage our parents' estate until we came of age, but, in truth, William cared for and raised me. Our relationship is more like a father and child than a sister and brother."

"Oh, Gwen, that's awful. I'm so sorry." Jane is by Gwen's side in an instant, giving her a hug.

When Jane releases her, Gwen offers a quivering smile to both of us, before schooling her face and digging further into the box of swimsuits. "It was a long time ago. And I really don't know anything about it except what William told me. I don't mind that he worries about me resuming my modeling career. He loves me. Ah, ha! Here it is."

She tosses a red bikini and a black cover-up dress to me. I want to ask why she didn't take up modeling again now that she's an adult and doesn't need permission. I guess I understand Darcy being protective of his sister after losing their parents at such a young age. But to prevent her from doing something she so obviously loves?

There seem to be two sides to Darcy, and they don't mesh. It makes me wonder what I'm missing.

CHAPTER 11

My eyes close and I soak in the late afternoon sun. Cameron set up a net across the pool, and Gwen and Jane are playing volleyball against Cameron.

To my relief, Darcy is sitting at a table with his laptop, fully dressed in a pair of knee-length shorts and a polo shirt that match the blue of his eyes. Not that anyone could see his eyes due to the screen he's been fixedly staring at for over an hour. At least, that's what I thought at first.

As I lounge on the chair, sunbathing, I swear someone is looking at me. It has to be Darcy but every time I open my eyes, there he is peering into that stupid computer screen, his lightly stubbled jaw line tense with concentration.

Poor outnumbered Cameron tried to convince Darcy to join in the volleyball game, but Darcy simply shook his head, typing away on his keyboard.

I hear the slapping of feet on the pavement. I open my eyes and see Gwen closing the lid to Darcy's laptop. "Seriously, you need to stop," she says staring pointedly.

He frowns. "Business doesn't stop, Gwen."

"But you can stop and celebrate with us. Come on Willie, play with the big kids and stop being such an asshat." She frowns playfully at him.

Darcy's gaze cuts to me, and I laugh, hands up. "I didn't teach her that! Don't look at me that way."

Gwen laughs and smacks his knee. "I've learned worse words, big brother. I made a flow chart! Would you like to see? The word at the very top of the list, the word a lady should never say, is cuh—"

Darcy's hands fly over Gwen's mouth. He stares at her like she's lost her mind. Gwen breaks free and giggles like crazy.

Cameron calls out, "I don't understand how you can still focus on work, William. Not with so many beautiful women around."

Darcy's blue eyes flick to mine but quickly flick away. My stomach flutters, and I wonder if he really thinks I'm attractive.

"My concentration is exceptional, and I'm highly skilled at multitasking—even if others appear to be lacking in that regard." Darcy is trying not to smile when he looks at Gwen, who is standing next to a fountain with her arm wrapped around the statue's neck like they're best buds.

"Are you still complaining about the board?" Gwen places her hands on her hips.

"I don't complain. I fix things."

Gwen turns to me, smirking. Holding out a hand, she says, "He's fixing things and doesn't have time for fun. You can melt on the pool deck, Will. In the meantime, Beth and I will be swimming."

"That's the best idea you've had all day."

"You just want my head underwater so I stop talking to you."

"Maybe." Darcy smirks at his sister. "Have fun. I'll join you when I'm finished." Darcy's voice is sweet and sincere. I doubt he'll finish in time to swim with her but he obviously adores her.

"You better!" Gwen runs toward the pool, jumps, and dives into the crystal water. Her head disappears beneath the surface and reappears moments later at the other end of the pool. "Beth!"

I sigh. William Darcy is skitzoid. He has to be. How else can he be such an ass one minute and so sweet the next? I'm not going to figure him out. He's just a sexy plaything—when he doesn't talk—and that's okay. I can live with that. Anyway, he hasn't said two words to me since our kiss under the tree.

Screw him.

I grab the bottom of my cover-up and pull it over my head. Shaking my hair out, I toss the dress onto the chair.

I hear shattering glass behind me. When I turn, Bea is running toward Darcy with a dishrag, helping him clean up the lemonade he spilled onto his laptop and shorts.

His blue eyes stare unabashedly at my chest.

Gwen's right. The bikini does make my boobs look awesome.

With a slight smile, I pad to the edge of the pool and dive into it.

CHAPTER 12

Later that night, after Jane is asleep, I use the code I got from Cameron earlier and wander back down to the pool. I sit at the edge and put my feet in the warm water, swirling it with my toe, creating patterns on the surface.

The moonlight is bright this evening. Its silvery rays illuminate the yard, making it easy to see the silhouette of a man pacing along the edge of the gardens. I watch for a moment, thinking it's Cameron, but when he turns, and I see his profile lit by the moonlight, I know it's Darcy.

What's got him so agitated? I watch him for a while. He takes twenty paces and stops, ticks things off on his fingers, grabs the hair at his temples, then repeats. After ten minutes or so, I feel like a voyeur. I shouldn't be watching this. He has no idea someone is out here.

I pull my feet from the pool and decide to walk closer, maybe check on him. When I get close enough for him to hear me, his back is to me. His shoulders bow forward, and he grips his neck like he's in pain.

"Darcy?" I say gently. "Are you all right?"

He rounds suddenly, his blue eyes wide with panic. His beautiful face is marred with worry. A slew of silent words pass between us, and then he's in front of me, his hands on the sides of my face, his touch light and tender.

"Beth, I..." his words die in his throat before his mouth comes crashing down on mine.

I can't do this again, but... God! This kiss. It's perfect—hot and heavy.

The idealist in the back of my mind is hitting me with a stick. 'You don't love him!'

I'm glad I don't love him. Whoever takes on this hot mess is crazy. For the moment, I'm his distraction. I know it, and it's okay. Darcy is the same for me. His firm muscles and magical mouth distract me from the uncertainty of my own life.

The kiss deepens, becoming frantic. I'm gasping for air as his mouth moves to my neck. My knees weaken and wobble, but before I can fall, Darcy scoops me up. He walks over to the pool deck and places me in the doublewide lounge chair, reclining it more as he lays me down.

Something I can't decipher flashes across his eyes. He stumbles over his words, before spitting out, "I'm sorry, Beth, I—"

Yeah, he's not walking away this time. I reach for him and pull his mouth to mine. There's a rush of heat as our bodies collide, filling me until every inch of my body is humming, throbbing, craving his touch.

Darcy's lips are hot and perfect as he kisses me deeper. His hands slip under my sweatshirt and along my side. He's careful, moving slowly, gradually toward my curves. I want him to feel me in his hand, to hold onto my breast and stroke my taut flesh. I flush as it happens, sucking in air so erratically that Darcy slows and looks up at me.

I close my eyes and tip my head back, afraid I'll ruin the moment. My body arches into his hand and the sensation of his skin on mine is divine. I know his eyes are on me, watching me writhe on the chaise in response to his touch.

I feel him lie next to me, shifting his weight so both hands can touch me. At first, I think he's going to stop, but he doesn't. His other hand finds my waist, sweeping over my other breast before dipping down lower. He leans close to my ear, whispering, "Tell me when to stop, Elizabeth."

I open my eyes and look up at him, wondering what he's going to do. His beautiful face is transfixed on mine, as he pinches my nipples gently between his fingers. My mouth opens, and I let out a silent gasp of pleasure.

I don't realize my hips are moving until his fingers slide beneath my waistband. His hand on my breast stills as his other hand runs along the seam of my core. I shudder beneath his touch, my lips parting and words flowing, begging for him to touch me.

"Beg me, Elizabeth, say my name." His voice is so deep, so fucking sexy. The desire to sit on those beautiful lips flashes through my mind, making me moan. I've gone crazy. I must have.

Breathlessly, I beg, "Touch me…" Which name? He doesn't like informalities, but I'm not calling him Darcy—not now. I lick my lips and open my eyes. His gaze is locked on my mouth, watching every movement. When I speak, his eyes darken, and a rush of exhilaration flows through me. "William. Please, touch me, William."

He rolls on top of me and moves his hands in a magical way. The hand on my breast caresses me in a way that makes my hips buck, but his other hand holds me down, gently stroking me. As he feels how wet he's made me, he groans in my ear. I can't hide how much I want him, and no longer want to.

I shift my hips, jerking them up toward his finger, forcing it inside me. I gasp, repeating the movement, over and over, faster and faster until I'm breathless and looking into his eyes. Darcy hungrily watches my hips buck into his hands and my head tip backward. I don't care if he sees me like this. I want him to see. I want him to know what he does to me, how it makes no sense and defies all logic. I stayed. I didn't run.

A rhythm develops as I push into his hand, and he pushes back. His lips part and I can feel his warm breath on my neck as my body winds tighter and tighter. Heat is dripping between my legs, and desire is twisting knots in my stomach. I'm so close. It's as if he can read my mind because he shifts his hand and presses another finger inside, allowing his thumb to rub against that perfect spot. I gasp, bucking wildly into his hand, as he begs me to come for him.

I can't hold it back anymore, and I don't want to. Every inch of me suddenly shatters in bliss. He slips his hand away, but remains next to me, looking down into my eyes. He smoothes the hair away from my face and softly asks, "Do you know what you do to me? Do you have any idea?"

I don't reply. Instead, I reach for him and bury my face in his chest, enjoying the feeling of being in his arms. I can feel mortified tomorrow.

CHAPTER 13

"Jane, stop worrying. This won't be the last time you see Cameron—that man adores you!"

The early morning light cuts through the windows of Jane's bedroom, as we wait for the car. Despite my best efforts, Jane is convinced Cameron will lose interest in her now that the mural is complete. For as happy as she was yesterday afternoon, today every fiber of her being radiates despair. Loose strands of hair escape her ponytail and curl against her pale cheeks, framing the sad eyes she keeps shooting my direction.

"I don't know." She bites her lip. "After whatever that was that happened yesterday by the pool between you and Darcy, he might not—"

"I didn't do anything!"

"Beth, Darcy is Cameron's best friend, and he doesn't seem to like us very much."

"Now you sound like Mom." If she could summon that tone with our Mother I'd worry less.

There's a knock on the door, and Bea pops her head into the room. "Miss Jane, your car has arrived."

"Thank you, Bea," Jane says. "We'll be down in a minute."

I zip my backpack and hook it over my shoulder. "I'll go out of my way to be nice to Darcy in the future." My cheeks involuntarily flame bright red when I think of how nice he was last night.

Jane has her back to me, and doesn't notice. "Goodness, don't do that. I think he likes baiting you. If you go out of your way to be nice, he'll think you like him." She giggles as she pulls her Versace garment bag over her shoulder. More of Mother's purchases.

"There's something about him that makes me want to—" I freeze at the sound of a sugary-sweet, high-pitched voice.

"Oh, no!" Jane's hazel eyes widen in terror. "It's Mother."

"I thought she was just sending us a car." Cameron's house may be huge, but Mother's voice carries. Darcy's going to hear everything she says from wherever he's hiding. I've not seen him since last night.

That's a little bit good and a little bit bad. When he loosens up, Darcy is...a stupid smile spreads across my lips as I'm thinking about him. Darcy is sexy, moody, and in need of a serious taming. I love fighting with him. I wish his business practices weren't evil. That part makes me wonder.

Mother's shrill voice carries through the halls again, and my back goes ramrod straight. I grab Jane's wrist and look out the second story window. "Let's jump and run like hell down the interstate. No one will notice."

Jane's mortification fades for a split second, and she laughs. "Stop it, Beth."

"Ugh! Fine. I'll play interference with Mother while you load our stuff," I say, grabbing the keys to Mary's motorcycle and jogging out the door.

"Mr. Bingley, I apologize for being unable to tour your lovely home earlier this week. Who was your decorator?" Mother talks so fast that she's not even coming up for air anymore. "I'm sure you had the best. My goodness, the chandelier is simply lovely. Is that real gold on the ceiling? I'm sure it is. Oh! Is that the Phoenix vase recently auctioned at Sotheby's? It's from the Yuan dynasty isn't it? It went for at least sixty thousand pounds, I believe, which is a sizeable sum of money in American dollars—nearly one hundred and twenty thousand, I believe."

I enter the room to see Cameron squirming in his seat while Mother rhythmically raises a steaming full teacup to her lips as if about to drink then lowers it, launching into another question instead.

She resembles an animatronics figure in the Hall of Presidents at Disney World, talking and moving whether anyone listens or not. Unable to help herself, Mother shares her opinions and observations about every single object in the room, pointing out how much money each is worth as if Cameron didn't know.

Cameron smiles politely, nodding in answer to her questions even though she doesn't pause to notice his response. When he sees me, his green eyes lock on mine, pleading for me to save him.

I stride into the room with my hands behind my back and a smile on my face. "Mother, what a surprise. We didn't expect you to collect us personally."

"Of course, I came. I'd be remiss without thanking Mr. Bingley for allowing you and Jane to stay as his guests."

"Please, Mrs. Bennet, call me Cameron."

"Only if you'll call me Victoria." She daintily places her cup and saucer back on the tray and slowly turns to me. "Beth, I've just heard more speculations that Michael Frey will officially announce his campaign for Senate soon. Has Colin mentioned—dear, Lord! What are you wearing?"

"Clothes?" I plop onto the seat next to her. I'm wearing the same jeans, black t-shirt, and leather jacket I wore when I drove over earlier in the week.

"I apologize for my daughter's attire," she says to Cameron with a twitchy smile.

He chuckles. "Victoria, she's been a tremendous help to Jane, and a delightful guest. It's been my pleasure having both of your daughters at my cottage this week."

"You're too kind. As I was saying, Michael Frey will announce his run for Senate soon, and I'm shocked to hear it first on CNN."

Colin must be dying somewhere. I need to call him.

Mother continues, "Our family and the Frey family have been friends for ages. I'm not sure if you know this, Cameron, but we lived in Dallas before we moved to New York."

You mean before we left New York the first time because you nearly bankrupted Dad's business. Daddy was forced to salvage what he could from an awful situation, and Texas' tax laws make it a debtor's haven. Temporarily relocating gave Daddy time to pay his debts without completely ruining us, while accessing a pool of high-profile investors unfamiliar with our reputation. Mother acts like it had nothing to do with her, but I know otherwise.

Mother beams, glancing from me to Cameron, "Beth and Colin were high school sweethearts."

I stare blankly across the room, knowing she won't let me speak, but it doesn't stop me from trying. "That's not true, we're just—"

"Now, Beth, please don't interrupt. You know how I hate such rude manners."

I fold my arms across my chest and keep quiet. As long as she's talking about me instead of the value of Cameron's antiques we're good. I sit back listening to Mother tell her version of my relationship with Colin.

"It broke Beth's heart to leave Colin when we moved back to New York. You should've seen the two of them, so darling together." She sighs. "Colin's mother, Andrea, said Colin was so devastated by Beth moving he hasn't dated any girls since."

That's because he's gay, but I don't mind Cameron thinking I'm a heartbreaker. He glances at me to confirm my mother's story. I cluck my cheek with my tongue and shoot a finger gun at him. You know it. I'm hot stuff. Bwuhahaha.

"Thank goodness for the internet," Mother continues as if an expert on Frey family affairs. "Even though Beth attended university in Texas and

Colin went to Harvard, they managed to have virtual dates all the time. And now that Colin and Beth are both back in New York, I'm sure he'll pop the question any day now."

I choke back a laugh. "What makes you think he'll do that?"

"Because Catherine Degatto told me the Freys are visiting New York next month. Why else would they travel so far if not to visit with you?"

"I don't know, maybe to visit Colin?"

"Well, yes, but also because they'll want to welcome you officially into their family."

Cameron is sweet. "Either way, it'll be nice for Colin to see his family again," he says.

"Can you imagine the boost their only son's engagement will provide Michael's Senate campaign?" Mother's eyes are on fire with excitement, but her face takes a sudden turn toward regret. "Oh, no! I've ruined it! Now, Beth, you must look surprised when he asks you."

"I will look utterly shocked when Colin asks me to marry him. Scout's Honor." I hold up three fingers with one hand and cross my heart with the other.

Cameron smiles, but doesn't laugh. He tucks his chin for a moment, and then nods as mother starts talking again.

"Catherine also mentioned hosting a masquerade ball fundraiser for Michael Frey. Will you attend, Cameron?"

Cameron blinks, surprised Mother's giving him a chance to speak. "Yes, of course. If you permit me, I'd be honored to escort your family and purchase the tickets for all of us."

"How wonderful. Jane will be delighted to hear that."

"Hear about what?" Jane's soft voice comes from behind us.

Cameron lets out a breath and his eyes grow soft as they look at Jane standing at the doorway. "Jane, you look lovely."

"Thank you," she says shyly.

"Cameron is accompanying us to the Degatto's next masquerade ball. Oh, and I'm getting married!" I let out a squeal and smile at her like the Joker.

"What?" Jane's brow pinches as her gaze darts between Mother and me.

"Girls, be serious," Mother admonishes. "Let's keep Beth's engagement to ourselves for now, shall we?"

Mother walks past Jane taking a moment to pluck a piece of lint from Jane's pink summer dress. "How lovely! At least one of my daughters has good taste."

As Jane and Mother slide into the car, I glance around. No sign of Darcy. Apparently last night was a one-time thing. I can't blame him—we have nothing in common. He lives and breathes on a different plane. But I can't help but wonder which man is real—the one with the cold eyes and snobbery, or the guy with the soft voice and caring touch.

CHAPTER 14

It's late in the evening, and I'm looking over Dad's accounts again. Dad's at a meeting, not due back for another hour. It gives me extra time to examine the dozens of Excel files Mary and I found in his computer.

The numbers don't look any better now than they did a week ago.

I reach for my coffee, sipping as I scroll through, pausing to scribble on my growing list of notes. The only way Dad will listen to me is to know everything inside out, and grovel a little—okay, a lot—for looking at the books in the first place. He clearly needs help. I'm not sure why he hasn't said anything.

"When you were little, you loved sitting on my lap while I balanced the books." I jump, startled by the unexpected sound of Dad's voice. "You thought all the red on the screen was pretty."

"That was before I knew what it meant. Dad, I'm sorry." I set my pen down and swivel my chair to face him, rubbing my eyes as they adjust to the darkness of the room.

Dad sits on the couch across from me. He's exhausted—dark circles rim his eyes, and his skin is yellow and gaunt. "You were always asking questions. Always trying to learn," he pauses, staring off into space, remembering the past.

"Yeah, I was a pest."

He smiles softly. "No, you wanted to learn. What father could deny his daughter of that? I remember when you couldn't figure out a problem, you'd get so mad, and your little face would scrunch up as if you could physically force the answer out. You're so different from your sisters, Elizabeth. Jane believed everything we told her without question."

"She still does," I interrupt in a mumble.

"Yes," he chuckles, "She does. And Mary, well, she changed when Sofia died. Mary will sort herself out in her own time. But you, you have this fierce independence, this determination to make your way in the world. You're so much like your mother."

"What?" I screech. "I'm nothing like Mother."

His brown eyes, so much like mine, gaze at me intently. His lips curve into a warm smile. "It's hard for you to believe, but your mother was different when we first married. Her priorities have changed."

"That's a bit of an understatement, don't you think?"

"Beth, you can't understa—"

"You're right. I don't understand." I move to sit by his side on the couch. "I know you love Mother. I know you want to please her, but you can't wear yourself out maintaining this lifestyle. We don't need it. We do need you."

He frowns. "Not everything is as it appears, Beth. You're too quick to judge."

"I know what I see, Dad. Sometimes, a cigar is just a cigar."

"What?" He looks at me, puzzled.

"It means I can't find any deeper meaning for Mother's actions other than her being a social climber."

He winces.

"Daddy, you have to tell Mother to stop spending."

His jaw locks and his face grows angry. It's an expression I haven't seen in a long time. "Elizabeth Bennet, we are your parents. The relationship I have with your mother belongs only to us, and I will not allow you to dictate how we live our lives. Additionally, you will show us the respect we deserve."

"But she can't go on spending like this—"

"No buts." His face softens when he sees tears forming in my eyes. "Beth, I know you care. There's just so much you don't know about what's happening."

"Then tell me." My voice is small.

"I can't. I can tell you that your mother and I have always put you and your sisters first. We love you."

"Oh, Dad." I throw myself into his arms, crying. "I have to do something. I can't stand idly by watching you suffer like this. Maybe I could help you in the office?"

He hesitates before answering. "All right. I could use a little help."

I let out a breath of relief. Somehow I'll find a way to convince him we need to cut back. My thoughts are cut short by the doorbell.

"Colin! What a surprise," I hear Mother say in a voice that doesn't sound surprised at all. "Come in, come in. Beth," she yells in a singsong voice, "Colin's here!"

"Good luck, kiddo. You better get in there before your mother starts taking Colin's measurements for his wedding tuxedo." He winks at me, humor twinkling in his eyes.

"Dad!" I laugh. "We're not getting married. There's no way Colin would ever ask me to marry him. We're just friends."

"I know. He's gay."

I do a double take.

He grins. "Don't look so surprised, I know things."

"How?" For a moment, I'm worried that it came from me.

"Beth," he places his hand on my shoulder and squeezes, "some things don't need to be said. To someone who knows that boy at all, something like this is obvious. But don't tell your mother—she'll be loudly disappointed." He stands, and winces. "I'm a bit tired. I'm going to take a quick nap. Give Colin my regards."

CHAPTER 15

By the time I reach the sitting room, Mother has Colin cornered, grilling him with rapid-fire questions. Jane's distressed face is flushed red with embarrassment, but Colin takes it all in stride. Being a politician's son is not without benefits.

"You must be thrilled your father announced his Senate campaign. Of course, he'll win by a landslide." Mother smoothes the skirt of her designer dress. It's new. Of course, it is. Fuck me sideways. If there's one thing the Bennets can do, it's go down in style.

"My family is very excited." Colin smiles.

"Now that you've taken residence in New York, are you considering a political career here? I suggest you start small first. Maybe run for mayor first, and then governor? Wouldn't that be wonderful, Jane, having the governor of New York as a close family friend?"

"Maybe," I interrupt, "Colin doesn't want to be a politician."

"Oh, Beth. Don't be ridiculous," Mother says as I sit down next to Colin. "Of course, he does. Who wouldn't?" She nearly giggles, but covers her lips before her composure can escape.

"Actually, Mrs. Bennet, I'd prefer to settle into my law career before considering other career moves."

"Speaking of settling," Mother's eyes jump from mine to Colin's like a Ping-Pong ball, "you'll want to marry soon, I'm sure."

"Mother." My tone is a warning.

"Maybe even start a family..."

"Mom!"

"Especially now with your father's campaign starting soon. Just think of the positive publicity your family could gain through a wedding! Wouldn't that be exciting?"

"MA! Stop! Leave things alone for once."

Her eyes flick to mine, and if she owned a gun, I'm pretty sure she'd shoot me right now. I'm 'that' child—the disobedient, willful, and defiant ingrate. If she could mount me above the fireplace and write a book about taming her wayward daughter, she would.

"Elizabeth, everyone with a respectable career marries. It's not a secret."

Colin shoots me a side-glance and intercedes on my behalf. "The media does love a good wedding."

We're saved from further wedding plans by the sounds of stomping feet and a slamming door.

"Colin Frey! Get your pasty ass out here!" Mary marches into the sitting room wearing ripped pants and black combat boots. She flops on the couch between us, tosses one tattooed arm around Colin's shoulder and uses the other to stab him in the chest with one finger. "Your ass is grass, golden boy!"

"Your hair... Your hair is... GREEN!" Mother cries, her face frozen in horror.

"Don't be silly, Mother. It's not green—it's lascivious lime," Mary draws out the 'L' with her tongue and grins before turning back to Colin.

Mother's face grows an alarming shade of purple, but Colin jumps in before she blows. "I like it. It's fun."

Mary doesn't care that she's in the blast zone. "Don't try to butter me up, Frey. Is it true your father is making a deal with Degatto Industries, agreeing to block any environmental bills that prevent doing business as usual?"

Colin's pale blue eyes blink innocently. "I don't know. My father doesn't ask my permission regarding either his business decisions or his political policies. He doesn't ask me anything, actually.

"Michael Frey is a man of integrity," Mother says in a shocked voice. "He'd never make a deal like that. Colin, I apologize for Mary's behavior. Please know her accusations do not reflect how we feel about you or your family."

Mary ignores her, studying Colin for a moment. Then she sighs and relaxes her arms. "You've never lied to me before. And Suzy, from Suzy Loves Poochies, has been known to exaggerate from time to time."

"Oh, dear God. Not that ridiculous blog again." Mother pinches the bridge of her nose. "Why don't we give Colin and Beth some privacy? I believe Colin wants to ask Beth a personal question."

I glance at Colin and mouth an apology. He already knows Mother is crazy, but she's exuding it ten fold today.

"No, it's okay, you stay here, Mother," I say, knowing it will be too easy for them to hear everything we say in the sitting room. "We'll go to Dad's office."

Before Mother can say another word, I grab Colin's hand and haul him off the couch.

"It was nice talking to you—ow! You're ripping my arm out of its socket." Colin rubs his shoulder. I push him through the door and glance down the hall, making sure that no one is near.

Closing the door, I rest my forehead against it. My head is pounding. There is way too much drama in this house.

CHAPTER 16

"Are you okay, Beth?" I feel Colin's hand rest gently on my back.

"Yeah, it's just taking me a while to adjust to the family again." Colin drops his hand, and I turn to face him. "So what did you want to—Colin Frey, what the hell are you doing?"

Colin is kneeling in front of me, his summer blue eyes gazing intently into mine through long, dark eyelashes. I notice streaks of lighter blond hair I hadn't seen before, woven through soft bangs on his forehead. We've been friends for so long I sometimes forget how handsome he is. I hold in a breath as he folds my left hand into his.

"Beth, you are my dearest friend. You've been with me through good times and bad. When I needed a shoulder to cry on, you were there. When I needed a dance partner, you were there. When I needed a boob to feel up, you offered me yours."

"Colin!"

"Shh! Let me finish. It may have slipped your notice, my dearest Beth, but my friendly affection for you has transformed into something more intense. I think, nay, I know I love you."

He drops my hand to pull a Cartier box from his pocket and opens it. A monster of a diamond glitters under the overhead lights. "Elizabeth Bennet, will you do me the honor of becoming my wife?"

His eyes hold mine. His face beams sincerity and hope. It's heart-achingly beautiful, and, just for a moment, I'm left breathless.

Then dread knots my stomach.

How is this possible? I think back on all the time we spend together—our endless chats, the way he holds me when we dance. Could he… Does he… love me? Like, LOVE me, love me? How did a gay guy somehow fall in love with me after all this time?

Tears spring into my eyes as I gaze at him. I'm not in love with him. He's waiting for me to say yes. I can't. I can't marry him. But I can't hurt my one true friend.

What do I do?

Suddenly, I notice his lips twitch slightly—a movement so small, I almost miss it.

"Oh, my God, Colin! You ass! You almost had me!"

He clutches his chest and theatrically falls to the floor. "You wound me, woman!"

I plop beside him, laughing so hard my belly starts to ache.

"Admit it," he gasps between laughs. "I was good. You believed I was in love with you."

I shove his arm playfully. "What's wrong with you? I felt so guilty I considered saying yes to avoid hurting your feelings."

"Really?" His eyes shine with hope as he sits up. "Because I wasn't kidding about you marrying me."

"Be serious."

"I am serious. My father called this morning— and you know that means it's important. He hasn't talked to me directly since the day he caught me with Brad Carter."

I nod.

Colin and I met Brad our freshman year of high school when Brad transferred to Texas from California. Brad was tall, tan, and gorgeous, his hair bleached by the sun—and he had a mad crush on Colin. With my help, Colin went on his first date and even had his first kiss that year.

Everything was great until Mr. Frey caught them in an awkward embrace. Colin's attempted cover story was that Brad was helping him practice for wrestling team tryouts, but really? Colin on the wrestling team?

Since then, Mr. Frey has spoken with Colin through his wife or his personal assistant, and only when necessary. Were Colin not so popular in both the media and the polls, he'd have been disowned.

"What did he want?" I ask while picking at my nail polish.

"He wants to announce our engagement."

"Who gave him the idea we're getting married?" It takes a minute before understanding hits me. "Aargh! It was my mother wasn't it?" That's why she's been acting so giddy and telling everyone it was only a matter of time.

Colin looks like someone is about to punch him. "Please don't get mad."

"You didn't! You wouldn't!"

His voice pleads for forgiveness. "Beth, I didn't mean for it to go this far. A persistent photographer scored a photo of me with Mateo at Six Degrees the other day. Mom freaked and called me. I had to calm her down, so I kind of maybe told her I was kinda maybe planning to pop the question."

My brow shoots up. "Kinda maybe?"

"Fine. I told her I had a ring."

"Colin!" I groan, gazing at the engagement ring. A stream of unladylike words blast my buddy until I'm out. I tug at my hair and stare at the floor with my head in my hands.

"Come on, Beth. We can do this. You're not with anyone right now, and it'll only be for a couple of years until Father settles into his Senate position. In the meantime, I can support you and your family. I know your father is about to lose everything, and I can fix it."

"You know about that? How?" I glance over at him. "I didn't even know that until this week."

"There's been talk, and you know how gossip practically knocks on my door and invites itself in." He takes a hold of my hand. "Brace yourself. I also heard your mother has taken out multiple loans without being able to make payments on them. The bank is considering foreclosing on this apartment."

"Damn it!" I make a strangled sound in the back of my throat.

"I can help you, Beth."

"Colin, I can't take your money."

"Would being married to me be so bad?"

"It would be a total lie."

"Not really. We love each other. Well, I love you."

"I love you, too." I lean over and kiss his cheek. "But this kind of love won't keep us happily married. You'll be miserable. What about Mateo?"

"I broke up with him." Colin sighs and lets his body drop back to the floor. He stares blankly at the ceiling as he speaks. "Mateo's family knows he's gay.

They're okay with it—they've always been okay with it. But—"

"I'm sorry, Colin."

He shrugs. "It is what it is. He doesn't understand why I can't come out. My family won't be accepting—especially not now with my father running for Senate."

"I know. I wish it weren't true, but I understand what you mean."

Colin trails off, tilting his head toward mine. "Will you think about it? Please?"

My heart aches for him. For as bad as my mother is, Colin's dad is ten times worse. He's going to end up living a lie his entire life.

Could I do this even for a couple of years? I'd do anything for him, but this?

"People will know it's a fake marriage."

He laughs. "Honey, welcome to the wealthy side of town. We're all about being fake. Besides, I almost convinced you. My acting is top-notch."

My mind drifts back to Darcy, wondering if anything could come of that. While I don't think so, I'm reluctant to close the door. This will look bad, like I was dating Colin while I was getting all sexy with Darcy.

"Beth?" He says my name softly and catches my eye. "Is there someone? I don't want to ruin it for you." After watching me for a moment, Colin presses his lips together. He's about to retract his proposal.

"I'll think about it, okay? It'll change things between us and set us on a path I'm not sure I want to be on. Does that make sense?"

"Yeah, it does. I also know you wanted one marriage and the forever package. I know this isn't it." He gestures to himself. "Will you wear the ring while you think about it?"

I glance at it again. It's an emerald-cut stone that's bigger than my nose. "How many karats is that thing? It's a brick."

He slumps back into the sofa and shrugs. "Most women want big boobs and big diamonds." I smack him in the face with a pillow. "It's 73 karats and insured up the ass. You can wear it, lose it, or make it into a nose ring."

"I'd have panic attacks every time I step out of the apartment. " I drop the black box onto his stomach. "Put that thing away before Mother sees it and snatches it."

"You don't have to—um, Beth?" He squints, peering over my shoulder. "Why is there a camera up there?"

I look up at a small dome-shaped object attached to the ceiling. I hear the soft hum of a motor, like a camera zooming.

Mary's disembodied voice comes from the ceiling. "Holy shit! Take the ring!"

"Mary, is that you?" I yell at the ceiling.

The camera tilts up and down slowly as if nodding. "You buttmunch! You were spying on me!"

"We can hock the ring and donate the money to charity," Mary says, speaking through the camera again.

"OMG! Have you been listening in on us the entire time?" We stare at the camera expectantly, waiting for a response, when suddenly the office door bursts open.

Mary's standing there breathless as if she ran all the way down the hall from her bedroom. "Maybe! Besides, I agree with Colin. People would totally buy it if you two got hitched." She gestures between us and offers her best "duh" face.

"How did a camera get in Dad's office?"

"I put it there to spy on his meetings with business clients."

"Mary!"

"Only the clients that experiment on animals, or pollute the Earth, or use children from third world countries to manufacture products..."

My jaw drops as Colin giggles next to me. "Mary Bennet!"

Mary doesn't seem fazed. "Okay, fine! I listen to all of them, but stop changing the subject! Just think of it, Beth! With Colin's access to the Frey Oil cash, we can use it for good and not evil. No offense, Colin. Not that evil wouldn't look good on you, because black is totally your color."

"Likewise, and no offense taken, future sis-in-law." He sits up, holding out his fist so she can bump it.

"No! No fist bumping! I only said I'd think about it."

Mary waves me away as she thumps Colin's fist companionably then helps him up. They talk animatedly, planning our engagement as if I wasn't here. "We have so much to do. We need a plan for making sure the media picks up on this. Maybe you can do a slow build so it won't seem out of the blue."

"That's a great idea. There'll be tons of press at the Degatto's masquerade ball."

"Hello? I'm standing right here, people. Not engaged," I say, wiggling my ring finger in the air. "Nothing here."

"That's good, but we need a venue before then," Mary says ignoring me. "I've got it. Let's go to Six Degrees."

"Great idea." Colin surveys the baggy t-shirt and jeans I'm wearing. "We need to get Beth into something slinky, though. It's a requirement of the Frey women to look hot."

"Wait, what? I'm hot."

"You are, sweetie," Colin explains kindly, "but not in a bangable kind of way."

"You've got more of a doin-the-librarian going on. Oh! I've got just the thing!" Mary takes off before I can protest.

Before I can blink, I'm wearing four-inch heels and a shimmering black spaghetti-strapped dress so short I'm afraid to bend down.

As I totter out of the house and into Colin's Aston Martin, all I can think is tonight is going to suck.

CHAPTER 17

Colin is right. As soon as I accept his waiting hand and slide from the car, we're overwhelmed by a bombardment of clicks and blinding flashes. The paparazzi swarm around us, blocking the entrance to the club. Through the bright explosions of light, a huge man with arms as big as tree trunks pushes through the crowd. Relieved, we allow him to usher us into the building.

Inside, a sea of bodies ebb and flow in time with the deafening music, enveloping us in motion. A grouping of tables and stools create a barrier around the corner bar, each forming a tiny island of refuge in the pulsing crowd of people.

Mary stands near a wrought-iron staircase leading to the lower-level dance floor. Her hands are on her waist, tapping black-polished nails on her hips as she scans the room. Her dress, the same lascivious lime color as her hair, has long sleeves cut into slashes perfect for displaying the tattoos on her arms. A similarly dressed cluster of neon-coated dancers motion for her to join them.

"I'll catch you guys later!" She heads in their direction.

"Do you want us to let you know when we leave?" As the question leaves my mouth, a gorgeous specimen of a man emerges from the group heading toward us. His smooth coffee-colored skin shimmers underneath the flashing strobe lights.

Mary's face lights up when she sees him. "He's here!"

"Who?"

"A friend."

She sucks in a breath when he flashes a sexy smile at her. "No, don't worry about me. I'll get a ride."

She's halfway across the dance floor heading toward the guy before I can say another word.

As Colin and I dance, I spot a few celebrities and models I recognize. I try not to get too star-struck when a lead singer from one of my favorite rock bands waltzes in with his entourage. Jon Ferro is opposite us with his cousin Bryan. The two heirs are Mary's age, maybe younger, and surrounded by a mob of women.

I sway with the rhythm of the music, letting the sound transport me to a happy place where I don't have to think. About anything. It's only me and the booming bass of the music pounding inside my chest. Colin's offer to marry me is looming over me like a wave about to crash on the sand. Something feels off, and I don't think it's just that Colin would be miserable living a lie. As it is now, he's depressed he can't be his true self—he hides his sadness well. He hides everything.

I wish the world could accept people the way they are, for who they are. My mouth has gotten me into more trouble than anyone else I know—and it's because I won't back down. While I'm not as crazy as Mary in how I take on the world, I still plan my battles and whack the shit out of things that make life suck. Women's rights, gay rights, glass ceilings, and the way our society treats the poor all piss me off. Those are intsa-angry spots. Press one and the beast comes out to bite your head off.

A tingling sensation pricks the back of my neck. Someone is watching me. I glance around the crowded dance floor. Couples dance close to each other, their slick bodies grinding, swaying to the music.

In a back corner, underneath a strobe light, I see him, his muscular shoulders propped against the wall. The light flashes a series of colors, turning his blonde hair red, green, blue, and then back to his natural color. He sips his drink, studying me from above the glass. Women pass, their eyes caressing his sensuous body. It's obvious they want him. The way Sexy Guy stands there proves he's used to the attention.

As the song ends and another begins, I turn my attention back to Colin. Sad eyes look over my shoulder. "What's wrong?"

He leans into my ear. "Mateo's here with his sister."

Following his gaze, I see an athletic figure dancing with a voluptuous, dark-haired girl. When he turns and spots Colin, a brilliant smile lights his face. Pale blue eyes lock with dark brown ones. I look from Colin to Mateo and back to Colin again. I've never seen him mope like this over anyone.

"Talk to him."

"What's the point?" His eyes remain glued on Mateo. "I'm marrying you. My relationship with him is over."

I stop dancing and take his shoulders in my hands. "Listen, I haven't agreed to your proposal yet, and…"

"Don't say it."

"I'm not convinced Mateo is wrong about telling your family. Sooner or later they'll find out—they always do. When it happens, you'll need people around you who love you."

"You said it." He gazes down at me.

"Yeah, I did. It needed to be said. Go." I nudge him in Mateo's direction. "Talk with him. I'll be at the bar if you need me."

He pecks my cheek. "You're the best fiancée ever!"

I work my way through the crowd, cursing as I attempt climbing the stairs in stilettos. Just as I reach the top, a wave of people bump into me. I flail wildly, grabbing hold of the person nearest to me. I glance up, realizing I'm clinging to Sexy Guy's arm. My stomach flutters as I gaze into his honey brown eyes. He's gorgeous. His chiseled, flawless face moves close to mine and, as his hot breath gently washes across my cheek, I lose the ability to speak.

"Are you okay?" His voice sounds like silk panties, caressing me in all the right places.

I blink, trying to get my hormones under control as Sexy Guy waits for an answer. That's when I notice the empty glass in his hand and a smattering of wet red spots on his shirt.

"I'm so sorry. I ruined your shirt." He chuckles as he watches my hands fly around searching phantom pockets for something to clean the stains. I eye a couple of red napkins on a nearby table. "Come on."

"What are you doing?" He laughs as I pull his arm, towing him out of the crowd.

"I need to soak up the liquid before it settles in."
I dab his well-toned chest. Damn! Is he solid
muscle? "Maybe we can save your shirt."

"Don't worry about it." He smiles. Even his
teeth are gorgeous. Sexy teeth, all the better to nip
me with. Stop it, Beth!

When I move to his abdomen, I feel his well-
defined six-pack. My hand lingers a little too long,
and his hand is suddenly over mine. "Not that I
mind, but I'd prefer to be on a first name basis with
the hot girl feeling me up."

The touch of his hand is searing. "Feeling you
up?" I laugh lightly. "Yeah, I guess I am. Sorry."

"I'm Grant. Grant Wickham," he says, gently
stroking my hand with his thumb. "And you are?"

"Beth Bennet."

"It's a pleasure meeting you. Can I buy you a
drink?"

I gaze into his stunning eyes. He's obviously
interested, and he looks harmless. Besides, Colin is
here, and Mary is around somewhere if he ends up
being a psycho and I need an escape plan.

"Sure."

"Great." He pulls out the barstool for me. "Have
a seat."

I should sit on his lap and skip the barstool
completely.

CHAPTER 18

Over drinks and small talk, I find myself mesmerized by the way his beautiful face moves as he speaks. He tells me about working as a stockbroker at a brokerage firm and about his family—how he was an only child until his parents adopted his brother and sister.

I tell him about my sisters, pointing to Mary as she leaves the club with her "friend," and describing Jane's artwork. When he mentions knowing Anne Degatto, I try hard not to gag. Does EVERYONE have a connection to the Degattos? I quickly change the subject.

"So, how long have you lived in New York?"

"As long as I can remember. You?"

"This is the third time in the past few years. I cut out twice and hightailed it to Texas. I have a freaky attraction to cows. It's nothing major."

He's swallowing his drink when I say that last part and chokes. Laughing, he asks, "Cows?"

"Uh, right, I mean cowboys. I like big boots. It's easy to tell things about a man from his boots." I'm teasing, and he totally gets it.

"Check it out," he lifts his foot from under the bar and points. "13DD, baby."

I smile coyly and lean in close to him. Grant mirrors my movement, so we're lip to lip. "My, my, what big shoes you have."

My lips part, inhaling the taste of his breath on my tongue. I can't believe I'm doing this. I hardly know this guy, but I can't help myself. Maybe it's due to the three drinks I had as we talked. Or maybe it's because he's a sexy hunk of a man riveted by my every word even as runway models sashay past our table. Whatever it is, I desperately want to kiss him.

"All the better to seduce you with." He grins and just as he's about to kiss me, there's a tap on my shoulder.

I turn to see Jane and Cameron behind me.

"Jane, Cameron!" My surprised smile quickly freezes.

Darcy is standing behind them. This is awkward. Now it looks like I'm sucking face with a stranger in a bar after getting fingered by the pool with Darcy, and all before I marry Colin. Holy shit. I look like a total skank.

Darcy's beautiful face is hard to avoid, but I manage. His black shirt is cut to fit his frame and show off his narrow waist. His dark hair is tousled as if he's been running fingers through it. Even from a few feet away, I can feel anger coming out of him in waves. His sapphire eyes blaze with blue fire—the hottest kind. The stubble along his rigid jaw line makes him look dark and dangerous. My eyes drift along his incredibly broad shoulders, down his muscled arms, to a perfectly manicured hand perched on his shirtsleeve.

Anne Degatto.

So why is Darcy shooting fireballs at me if he's still with Anne? What a twat.

"I need to talk with you," Jane says in a rushed whisper.

"Let me introduce you to my new friend. Grant, this is my older sister, Jane. Jane this is—"

Before I know it, she's yanking me away from the table, speaking quickly. "Nice to meet you, Grant. I need to steal my sister away for a moment."

"I'll be right back!" I stumble as Jane takes me a few feet away from the table. "What the hell is wrong with you? Did you see him? He's hot, like holy fucking hell, hot!"

"I'm sorry. I didn't mean to be rude. I was worried."

"About what?" There's a sheen of sweat on her brow and a flush on her cheeks. I press the back of my hand against her forehead. "Are you sick? What's going on?"

"No, that's from dancing. We've been here for a while. Cameron brought us. Gwen wanted to come, but Darcy wouldn't let her come alone." She tilts her head in the direction of the dance floor where Gwen is being her gorgeous self. My eyes pop out as I see she's dancing with Jon Ferro. Way to go, Gwen! He's a little young for me, but perfect for her.

"We ran into Mary on our way in, and she told us where you were sitting. I wasn't going to interrupt you, but when we realized you were with Grant, Darcy kept watching you, worried."

"Psh," I wave a hand at her. "There's nothing to be worried about."

"Listen! Darcy is Grant's adopted brother. I didn't think anything of it until Grant touched you and Darcy nearly exploded. You should've seen him, Beth."

Awh, he does care.

"He's too late. Why does he care now? He's been here for hours—"

Jane interjects, "An hour."

"—watching me dance—"

"Not in a stalkery way, Beth."

"—and didn't bother to come over and say hi! Who does that? Who does that with a woman and then doesn't say hi? Fine. I'm mad. If he doesn't like Grant, that sucks for him."

Jane blinks, her eyes cut side to side, and she leans in. "I think I missed something."

I throw up my hands and glare at Darcy. "So did I! Jackass!" I squeak when I see Darcy make a beeline for Grant. "Hell, no. This isn't happening."

Cameron is standing between Darcy and Grant, smiling but fearful. Grant's expression is smug as he talks to his brother. Darcy's expression grows darker by the moment, and enough tension laces through his jaw that it barely moves as he speaks. I can't hear the conversation, but I see Darcy's lips form my name. Grant throws his head back in a laugh and sits back down at the bar.

Bunch of stupid fucktards can't keep their shit to themselves for one freaking night. I just wanted a couple of hours of mindless fun. Is that too much to ask?

Yes, yes it is. Grrrr.

I smile placidly and place my fingertips on the table. "Boys."

Darcy glares at me—it's an I-hate-you stare magnified to the tenth power. "Miss Bennet."

"I've just been catching up with my brother," Grant says, shooting me a sexy smile as Jane walks up behind me. "I hear you two have already met."

"Rather intimately, yes." I hold Darcy's gaze as I speak. "Apparently that was a handshake, though, because I never saw him again. My mistake."

Darcy's eyes narrow to slits. He's livid! Him! He doesn't even say anything!

Cameron laughs an octave too high. "Beth and Jane are dear friends, so of course they've met William."

"William is one of a kind." Grant says with an air of sarcasm in his voice. "Jane, it's been a pleasure meeting you. You're just as lovely as your sister."

"Thank you?" She looks at me questioning. Leaning in close to my ear, she hisses, "Handshake? I can't believe you said that out loud. Does that mean what I think it means?"

I frown. I want to yell out, I HATE EVERYONE! LEAVE ME ALONE! But I can't. Darcy is shooting lasers out of his striking blue eyes, and Cameron looks like he's going to puke. Meanwhile, Jane is wondering if she's been shaking hands properly.

I look to Grant, beseechingly. He catches on. "Now, if you don't mind, I haven't had a chance to dance." He holds out his hand. "Shall we?"

OVER YOU

I reach for my glass and toss back the amber liquid. Slamming it down on the table, I say, "Hell, yes."

CHAPTER 19

I feel Darcy's eyes follow me onto the dance floor. The pulsing music blares over the speakers. I swing my hips, moving to the beat. Grant's behind me, his hands on my hips. I place my hands on his hands, swaying in rhythm with him. With each move we make, his toned body presses into me until I feel his hardness against my back.

Lifting my hands off his, I weave my fingers through my hair and then into the air. I'm waving my arms, moving my body, inviting him to touch me. Grant's hands drift up my waist, his fingers brushing the sides of my breasts. I bite my lip in response to the heated sensation. His touch slowly glides down my waist again and skims my bare thighs.

I reach back and clutch the back of his neck. He dips his head, brushing his lips against my earlobe, against my throat. I suck in a breath, wondering if this is a good idea. The last guy I kissed ditched me. I can feel his stalkery gaze burning a hole in my back.

With everything going on, I just want to forget for a little while. Does that mean I'm a bad person? I don't see Darcy asking to cut in. Hell, he didn't even talk to me after the poolside pat down, which is too bad. I would have liked that.

No, Beth, stop it. I don't want to wallow in the past. I think that's a huge part of what's wrong with this family—we don't move forward. So we have no money. So what? We have each other, and that's what matters.

I'm not going to live my life looking backward and longing for what could have been. I refuse.

I have a hot guy who's into me right here, right now, and he's giving me his undivided attention. I should do the same.

The quick beat of the bass hammers into my chest, pulling me back to the present. The combination of music and touch are intoxicating. The spinning lights make me dizzy, drunk with sensation. It's a familiar feeling, one I feel too rarely.

What about love? The voice in the back of my head keeps nagging. You said you'd only kiss a guy you loved. You said you'd only sleep with a man who loved you back. What the hell are you doing!

Inner Me sounds shrill, as she beats my brain with one of the books I've read. Past mistakes and heartbreaks flash behind my eyes, and I realize that nothing turns out the way I plan. It doesn't matter if there's love or not.

And it won't matter tonight. I'm breaking my rule. Fuck it.

Grant spins me around, and I'm between his legs with his hand on the small of my back. Ordinarily this kind of dancing would send me running the opposite direction, but not tonight. My pulse quickens as his hips grind against mine, his honey brown eyes growing dark with desire. I place one arm on his shoulder, the other finding its way low on his back.

The singer's voice drifts through the club asking if the rumor is true, if the man loves her, daring him to touch her. For some reason, I look over Grant's shoulder searching for Darcy.

When I find him, he's standing alone, his arms folded across his broad chest. His handsome face is a mask under the flashing strobe lights. His eyes lock with mine for a moment, and I catch my breath. Then, suddenly, his head jerks to the left as if something caught his attention. His eyes widen with alarm, and he quickly charges through the crowd.

I turn to see what could cause him to freak out like that. Gwen's still dancing with Jon Ferro, gripping his shoulders and laughing as he tries to hold her up. Oh, no! She looks drunk.

Darcy clutches her arm, and she scowls. She slaps his hand away and tries to leave. She stumbles and Darcy catches her. Jon tries to speak, but Darcy ignores him, placing an arm under Gwen. Her face contorts with rage, and she's beating his arm, but Darcy ignores her, dragging her from the dance floor against her will.

No matter how drunk she is I don't think dragging her from the club like a fit-throwing toddler is the right thing to do. Poor Gwen. How does she tolerate him?

When they reach the top level of the club, Anne meets them. I want to slap that self-righteous look off her face. As if she never drank a little too much, a little too fast. Add in the condescending sneer and I'd like to pull her hair out.

Darcy whispers in her ear and Anne quickly goes to the table where Cameron and Jane are sitting. Cameron and Jane get up from their seats immediately and follow Anne out the door. I wonder if I should intervene, but she's not my sister. Their solution isn't bad, just embarrassing. I frown, trying to think of some way to help Gwen, but come up with nothing. Since Jane left with them, I know Gwen is in good hands. Cameron is sweet, too, and will make sure Darcy doesn't do something stupid.

"What's wrong?" Grant yells over the music, noticing the irritation on my face. His hot body moves seductively against mine, barely touching, teasing me.

I suck in a shaky breath and say what I've been thinking all night. "Nothing's wrong. Would you like to go someplace more quiet?"

His lips curl into a sexy smile. "I'd like nothing more."

CHAPTER 20

We've barely stepped into Grant's penthouse high above the city before he spins me around and pins me against the door, kissing me deeply. As if of their own will, my hands slide up his hard chest, touching, feeling, making me dizzy. I might be a little drunk. It's been too long since I've been with anyone and I'm desperate for his skin to meet mine.

I frantically work the buttons of his shirt, stripping it away and revealing taut muscles underneath. I trace the firm cords of his chest, drifting teasingly down, further, further, until my fingertips dip along the waist of his belt. He moans, pressing his hardness against my stomach.

A tingle sparks along my spine as his lips trail down my neck. When he reaches my shoulder he pauses, shifting the fabric of my dress over the swell and down my arm.

His lips sweep across my collarbone in the opposite direction, displacing the fabric from my other shoulder. I lift my arms slightly, letting the dress cascade down my body to pool my feet.

His eyes simmer with lust, drinking in the fullness of my breasts in the lacy black bra and trailing down to my matching panties.

Unable to survive the pause, I shove him onto a nearby couch and straddle him, moaning as his hands slide up my waist to my breasts, stroking and caressing them. I grind into him, loving the feel of his body and the delicious friction as he moves his hips in rhythm with mine. His fingers tug one bra cup, freeing the contents within, and his tongue flicks out, teasing my nipple.

I gasp at the contact as my body aches for him more. The rocking of my hips becomes more frantic as I grind against him, wishing away the clothes between us. My hands weave into his soft hair, and I pull him against me. He takes my exposed breast into his hot mouth.

A pinging sound comes from beneath me. I pause. Is that my phone? Who would text me now?

"Don't stop." His voice is deep and seductive. The commanding tone is enough to melt me.

I do as he says and keep moving against him. As he teases my breast, his hand slides between us. He's fumbling with his zipper when I hear the pinging again. The sounds come one after the other. I stop. Now it's his phone. What the hell?

"Maybe you should check that." I don't want to, but it's chiming like crazy, one after another.

"It's nothing important," he murmurs as his fingers continue to fumble at his waist.

He tries to kiss me again. I shake my head, as a sudden fear enters my thoughts. What if something happened to Dad?

"Maybe something happened?"

"I highly doubt that." His voice sounds aggravated, and he groans as I shift my weight to stand in front of him, waiting for him to check his messages. I stiffen at the cold look he gives me. Then, as if I'd imagined it, I blink, and his eyes are warm honey brown again. "But I'll check if it eases your mind." He smiles like he means it.

I nod and lift my phone. It's Jane. Nothing about Dad, just something about Grant. I don't bother reading the rest. I press the button on the top of my phone to kill the screen. This is why I don't tell people anything. They're so nosy. It's my rule. I can break it if I want to.

Grant swears under his breath. "Darcy, of course."

That's weird and a mile past being a voyeur in the club. "What does he want?"

"William and I aren't on the best of terms. He's just being a dick." He types something back, but before he can shut off the phone, another message comes pinging in.

When he reads the screen, his handsome face sours with anger. "Fuck him!" He types furiously into his phone.

I scan the room for my dress. This evening is not going as planned. "What's wrong?"

He smiles apologetically. "I'm sorry. I can't do this right now. Family problems."

Is he throwing me out? Seriously? "Should I go?"

"No. I want you to stay." He stands, kissing my cheek gently. His voice softens. "Why don't you pour yourself a drink, okay? I'll be right back."

I'm starting to remember why I don't sleep with guys that I don't know. This feels strange. I'm assuming it's normal brotherly crap, and Darcy is most likely being an ass about whatever it is. What were the odds that I'd go home with his adopted brother?

Grant tosses his phone on a console table and heads for the bathroom, picking up his discarded shirt on his way. After a few moments, I hear the sound of water running. What the hell just happened?

CHAPTER 21

I sigh in relief as I find my dress. If Colin were here, he'd tell me to forget my clothes and jump Grant in the shower. Hell, he'd probably do that himself if he weren't so much in love with Mateo. I saw the way Colin gazed into his dark eyes. At least for tonight, getting married to keep up appearances was all but forgotten.

Slipping my dress on, I pad to the kitchen and rummage through the brushed steel refrigerator for a bottle of water. As I drink, I walk through the living room. The shades of gray and black lend a modern, masculine vibe to the room. A hugeass flat screen TV rules the room from a dark gray wall, its court a u-shaped arrangement of neutral-colored couches.

As I glide my hand over the material of a soft gray throw pillow, my eyes land on Grant's phone. Curiosity and good manners war within me. My fingers slide over the console's sleek surface and pause over the phone. I really shouldn't look at it. It's an invasion of privacy. I listen to Grant's movements. The water's still running. Mary would do it. In fact, she wouldn't even bother being sneaky. She'd just snatch it out of his hand.

I'll take quick peek. That's all. He probably has it locked anyway.

My heart pounds as I snatch the phone. With a flick of my finger, the screen lights up. I scowl as I read the preview of his last text.

I quickly open his text messaging app and scroll through it.

WILLIAM: I meant what I said
WILLIAM: Stay away from the girl
WILLIAM: There will be consequences
GRANT: fuck off
WILLIAM: of which your parents will disapprove
GRANT: Fine.

Then there are more curses and threats. What the hell? I've caught me a crazy man. Darcy is insane. I sit down on a stool, place the phone back on the console, and stare into space.

"Beth, I'm sorry I snapped at you."

I scurry over to a couch and plaster a fake smile on my face. When he enters the room, I try to focus my attention on Grant rather than his crazy-ass brother.

"That's okay. I totally get family problems. You should meet my mother. She's a handful." Poor Grant. It must've been hard growing up in the same family with Darcy. At least, Gwen turned out okay.

He grins. "I bet my brother can top your mother."

"There's an image I never want to see."

Grant laughs as I make a face. "Seriously, though, William's the adopted brother you were telling me about?"

"Yeah, he's the guy."

I study him as he brushes a hand through his blond hair. He's debating whether or not to tell me more. The curious part of me wants to know why Darcy's such a dick and how people as sweet as Gwen and Cameron put up with him. I soften my expression and try to get him to open up.

"You don't sound too enthusiastic when you say that."

Grant's lips curl into a smile. "You've met him. What do you think?"

I've more than met him and think he's crazy. I can't say that, so I hedge. "I see your point. I just thought, since he's your brother, he'd be a little nicer to you."

"His idea of being nice is getting my parents to disown me rather than kill me."

"He what?"

"It's a long story," he sighs and rubs his temples.

"I've got time."

He heads to the bar and pours a drink. "Gwen is the only girl in our family, so everyone doted on her—you've met Gwen, haven't you?"

"Yeah, she's great." I fold my legs underneath me, getting comfy on the couch.

"Isn't she? William felt my parents loved Gwen and me more than him." He pads back across the room to sit beside me. "That's not true, you know. My parents were very sensitive to William and Gwen's needs. For the first few years after they moved in, it was like I didn't exist."

I touch his arm lightly. "That's awful."

His eyes grow sad for a moment, and then he shakes it off. "It was hard for me. I was only five when Mr. and Mrs. Darcy died. Gwen and I were close growing up. William didn't like that either. He's always been protective of her."

Psychotically possessive would be more of an accurate term. I nod, encouraging him to continue.

"It got worse when Gwen was approached by a modeling agency. My parents consented to her doing some modeling. I was even willing to help out. I went with her to some of the shoots when my mother couldn't go. William got jealous and asked her to quit modeling altogether. At first, she refused. Then, mysteriously, she started losing gigs. Gwen booked shoots increasingly less frequently, as if someone was intentionally sabotaging her career. Then, when we saw the images from this one particular job, William lost it. He completely overreacted to the ad, saying it was too revealing. In truth, it was tastefully done. Gwen looked beautiful. But there was no convincing him. He demanded she quit. I don't know what he told her, but she did."

"That's awful."

He takes a sip, shaking his head. "He has a lot of power over her. She was just a baby when she lost her parents, and William is her only biological family left. I can understand wanting to stay on good terms with him, but she needs to tell him to fuck off. I told her I'd be there for her, that she didn't have to quit, but she couldn't do it. She couldn't—or wouldn't—stand up to him. That's when she started drinking."

The rumor Rivas mentioned was true. And it's Darcy's fault. "That's horrible!"

"I know. It's awful. Gwen is drunk almost all the time. On most days, she can't even walk straight. William doesn't care. He wants her that way so he can control her."

"That's terrible. I can't imagine how hard that was for her—and you."

He smiles. "You think that's bad? You haven't heard what he did to make my parents disown me."

"There's more?" I ask, shocked.

"After he took Gwen away, William convinced my parents to trust him with their financial holdings. He liquidated their entire portfolio and invested the money in a Ponzi scheme. My parents almost lost everything! They didn't want to believe it at first. When they confronted him, he blamed me. Can you believe that? It's only because of me my family has any money left at all."

"Don't tell me they believed him?"

He lets out a breath. "Yes, they did. He's smart. He had everything planned out with a paper trail leading directly to me. Don't ever get on his bad side. He'll bring your entire family down, too."

"I'm so sorry this happened to you." I place my hand over his. His handsome face looks so distraught. How horrible to be shunned by your family—and under false pretenses. "Believe me, I won't let William Darcy anywhere near my family."

CHAPTER 22

I glance in the mirror at Mary's reflection. She's sitting on my bed, leaning against the headboard, watching as Jane and I get ready. "I can't believe you managed to get out of going to the Degatto's fundraiser ball."

"I think her orange hair might've had something to do with it." Jane lets out a soft laugh. "I was really hoping you'd come with us to this one, Mary. Cameron loves it when you go out with us."

Over the last few weeks, Cameron and Jane have been inseparable. If they aren't going out to a club or taking a stroll in Central Park, they are talking on Skype. On occasion, Mary accompanies them when they go dancing with the intention of digging up dirt on Bingley Tech. She was originally skeptical of Cameron, not believing anyone as wealthy as he is could truly be nice or have honest business practices. He must've convinced her, though, because she

~165~

emailed Suzy from Suzy Loves Poochies and told her to take down her blog post accusing Bingley Tech of outsourcing to third world countries.

"There'll be a lot of politicians present tonight, and it's a masked ball. You can verbally bash them without revealing your identity, but only if you wash out your carrot top." I grin and gesture toward her hair.

"Tempting," Mary says arching a brow and tapping her forehead with a pencil. "But nope, not tonight. I've got a date."

"Really? He must be someone special if you're missing out on an opportunity like this."

She focuses on picking the polish from her nails, avoiding my eyes. "Maybe."

"Uh, huh." I slide siren red lipstick across my lips.

"You'll miss wearing the gorgeous dress Gwen sent you." Jane lifts one of three evening gowns lying on the bed. A waterfall of glittering Swarovski crystals rain in carefully arranged lines from the waist transforming the full skirt into a dew-kissed spider web. "You would look awesome in this one."

In preparation for Degatto's ball, Jane and I had pooled our money to rent the cheapest dresses we could find. When three boxes of designer gowns arrived last week, we thought Mother had totally lost her mind. I was seconds from angrily calling her out when I noticed a note from Gwen inside one of the packages explaining that they were from her modeling days, and she thought they'd look beautiful on us.

My red gown fits perfectly. The strapless hourglass shape emphasizes my silhouette and the heart shaped bodice makes the girls look awesome—it even has a high slit perfect for dancing.

"It's an awesome gown," Mary admits, waggling her eyebrows at me mischievously. "I'll wear it to Beth's engagement party."

"Colin and I are not getting married. I can't do that to him. It seems like a major misstep. Besides, you know how I feel about marriage—it's forever. Colin's not the right guy."

"'Cuz he's super gay. He needs a cape." Mary teases and grins at me.

"Don't tell Mother any of that," Jane says, unrolling curlers from her hair. "She's already interviewing wedding coordinators. She'll flip out."

Mary nods in agreement with Jane. This situation has been difficult. I want to be there for him, but this isn't the right way to do it. Colin is so busy, both with work and with helping coordinate Catherine's fundraiser for his father, we haven't had a chance to talk. Not that I've been searching for one. The longer I can avoid agreeing to his proposed mock marriage, the better.

There's a loud thud at the window followed by a squawk and frantically flapping wings.

"What is that?" Opening the window, Mary peaks outside. "Oh, no!"

"What's wrong?" I ask.

"Get me a box, hurry."

I go into the closet and grab an old shoebox. When I turn, Mary has a pigeon cupped in her hands.

"The poor thing." Jane gently strokes the pigeon's tiny head with her finger.

"What's wrong with her?"

Mary lifts the pigeon's feet to examine them. "She looks hurt, and there's a string tangled around her feet. I'm taking her to my room to try to get it off her. Do you have some antibacterial cream? Her feet look infected."

"Yeah, in the medicine cabinet."

She smoothes the bird's feathers and speaks in a soft, calm, very un-Mary-like voice. "There, there, Lucy. I'll fix your little feet right up."

I laugh. "You're naming her already?" Mother doesn't allow pets. Despite the rule, Mary snuck rodents, lizards, and even an armadillo into our house while we were growing up, claiming them all as pets.

"She looks like a Lucy, don't you think?"

"I think you shouldn't get too attached. And hide her! Mother will freak if she finds a pigeon in the apartment," I yell as she leaves for her room.

"Oh, goodness. I didn't realize how late it is." Jane rushes to the mirror, brushing her hair furiously. "Cameron and Colin will be here in ten minutes."

"Are you sure Darcy's not going to the ball?"

After speaking with Grant, I've stayed as far away from Darcy as possible. Grant hasn't tried to contact me since our night together. It really irks the hell out of me that he listened to Darcy's threats, but I've been so busy working in Dad's office, I decided to let it go. Grant was attractive, but not worth the drama it would cost to continue seeing him—especially if Darcy makes things difficult for Jane and Cameron because of me. Jane is too happy with Cameron. I can't mess that up.

"I'm pretty sure. Cameron said he's in San Jose on business." She slips into her champagne-colored gown, instantly looking Grace Kelly beautiful. "I still can't believe what Grant told you about Darcy. He may be a little standoffish—"

"A little?"

She giggles. "Okay, a lot. Still, I can't imagine him doing something so cruel, especially to his own family."

I sigh, gathering my dress. "That's because you see only good in people. Can you do the zipper?"

"It's more than that. Darcy seems to take so much pride in doing what is right. I can't imagine anyone who values common decency and good character investing in a Ponzi scheme and then lying about it. It's out of character."

I snort. "What you consider right and what he considers right are two different things. Who do you think he'd claim has the correct way of thinking?"

"My turn." She places herself in front of me. "You may be right. But if what Grant says is true, I can't believe Cameron would be friends with someone like Darcy."

"Maybe he believes Darcy's lies?"

"They've been such close friends for a long time. Cameron would know if Darcy was lying." She pauses, her concern written in her eyes. "Please don't be mad, Beth, but what if you're wrong about Darcy? Is it possible Grant is the one who lied?"

Yeah, right. "It's much easier for me to believe Darcy duped Cameron than to believe Grant lied. You can't make up things like that on the fly, and you didn't see how he looked when he spoke. He was sincere, his voice still feeling the pain of betrayal. There's no way he lied."

"I don't know . . ."

Reaching into a small bag, I pull out black Venetian masks lined in colors that compliment out gowns.

"Come on, this is something I do. It's my thing. I can tell when people are lying. I've always known."

Mary chimes in, "She has. It's like she has a lie detector soldered into her brain."

Jane sinks onto the edge of the bed, slipping on her shoes. "All of this is so disturbing. I don't know what to think, Beth."

"You should know exactly what to think, you just don't want to admit it—Darcy is a prick."

Her eyes shoot up to meet mine, and I immediately regret my words. It's not fair to push Jane like that. She loves Cameron, and Darcy is his best friend. It makes sense she'd want to see Darcy in a good light.

"I'm sorry. I didn't mean to bitch at you." I push off the bed and link her arm with mine. "Come on. Let's wait for the limo in the lobby, and I promise if I run into Mr. Darcy again, I'll try to be nice."

As we walk out of the apartment, she says, "I'm so glad you're giving William a chance. He isn't that bad. I think he's just shy."

I throw my head back and laugh. "Now, that's what I find hard to believe. A man in charge of a multibillion-dollar empire, shy? Yeah, right."

"I think he is. Did you know he doesn't know how to dance?"

"No way!"

"He knows the basics. Nothing fancy. After the charity gala, he asked me for my dance instructor's phone number."

We reach the lobby just as the limo pulls up. Colin and Cameron step out, both looking gorgeous in their tuxedos.

"Who asked? Cameron?" I watch him rush to open the glass door for us. His handsome face lighting up as Jane walks out.

"No. William."

CHAPTER 23

The ballroom looks like a page from a storybook. Masked women float on elegant clouds of tulle while masked men in inky black tuxes slip fluidly through the maze of ball gowns.

As Colin escorts me in, the first person I see is Anne Degatto standing next to her mother. Even behind a diamond-studded mask, an unforgiving expression dominates her face. She's a perfect reflection of her mother.

Cameron leads Jane to the dance floor, whisking her away with a graceful swish of skirts. I stand with Colin, drinking champagne and watching Jane's fairy tale unfold. Across the ballroom, I'm relieved to see Mother and Daddy sitting at a table talking with his golfing buddy, Dr. Brandon. Asking him to dance will provide the perfect ruse to discuss Dad's health, and I make a mental note to do so later. If anyone can convince him to see a specialist, it's Dr. Brandon.

"Colin Michael Frey!" Andrea Frey's face pinches into a scowl. She marches to us, her light gray gown fluttering as she moves.

"Mom looks angry. Hide!"

"It's too late, Colin. She's already seen us," I whisper, wondering what crawled up her ass.

Andrea Frey stops abruptly in front of us. Pale blue eyes so similar to Colin's regard me coldly through a hand-held silver-sequined mask. She purses her lips, her eyes scanning my body, and resting uncomfortably on my chest. She's so angry, the plume of white feathers on the side of her mask is vibrating.

"How could you? How could you do this to your father?" She hits Colin in the back of his head with her open hand. "Your engagement is about to be announced, and you bring this woman to his fundraiser. God, Colin, the media is right outside the doors. What were you thinking? And what about poor Beth? She'll be devastated when she finds out. Tell me you and your America's Next Top Model floozy entered through the back door. Tell me this disaster isn't already on the news."

"Mom, please, let me explain. This is—"

She hits him again. "I won't hear your excuses. This isn't the time or place to be flaunting a conquest."

I bark out a laugh. Holy crap! She doesn't recognize me.

She throws me a death glare. "Keep laughing, missy. I'll deal with you in a minute!" She waves her hand at me dismissively, redirecting her rage at Colin. "As much as your father might be pleased to finally see you with a woman like this," she sneers the word, "you take her out of here this instant before anyone else sees you together."

"Mrs. Frey, it's me, Beth."

Her eyes widen with shock. Reaching into her silver clutch, she takes out a pair of glasses. "Beth, dear. Is that you?"

"Last I checked, yes." I lift up my mask for a moment and smile at her.

"Oh, my dear girl, you startled me. You look so…so different." She leans in and says in a not-so-quiet whisper, "Your breast implants look convincing—though they are a tad too large. Nothing that can't be corrected."

"Mom!" Colin's face turns beet red. He looks cute when he's embarrassed.

I'm trying not to turn the same color as my dress. I lean in and quietly whisper, "They're real."

She pushes up her glasses, continuing to stare at my chest. "Well, now, you are a late bloomer. May I say that the bodice of your dress—"

"Mom, can we please talk about something else," Colin says, exasperated.

"Oh, yes." She places the glasses back into her clutch. "Victoria is looking well these days. You must give me the name of the surgeon who did her work. And that beautiful choker she's wearing. She got that from Sotheby's auction last week, didn't she? I'd been eyeing that necklace for myself."

I try not to roll my eyes as she lists all the expensive antiques, jewelry, and furs she recently acquired. My mother and Andrea Frey are almost the same—their only difference being the Frey Family still has money.

"So, where is it?" She eyes my left hand, expectantly.

"Where's what?"

"Uh, Mom. I need to talk to you in private." Colin attempts to take her aside.

"Not now, Colin." She waves him off. "The ring. Where's the ring? Colin said you two were engaged and—oh, no. Don't tell me he hasn't asked you yet?" Her eyes grow wide.

Aw, crap! I'd forgotten Colin told her he bought an engagement ring. I didn't want to do this now. Colin's face is pleading. I sigh, placing a fake smile on my face. "We wanted tonight to be Mr. Frey's night. We're all so proud of his running for Senate."

"Oh, how sweet of you! Don't worry, dear. I won't say a thing until you two are ready to make the formal announcement."

"Yes. Yes. That's nice, Mom. I think I see father waving you over. Come on, Beth." Colin pulls me to the dance floor so fast I stumble trying to keep up with him.

"Don't be mad at me," he says as we begin to dance.

"Colin, how am I going to get out of this one? What if your mother talks to my mother? What if she confirms our engagement? Your mom may be able to keep a secret, but mine can't. She'll have our engagement announcement running across the news ticker in Times Square."

He laughs. "She wouldn't do that."

"Have you met my mother?"

His face turns serious. "Okay, so maybe she would, but you have nothing to worry about. My mom may be flakey, but she keeps her word. For now, could you just pretend to be madly in love with me?"

"Colin, this is a bad plan—"

"Please, Beth."

"It's not right, we'll both be miserable, and—"

"Please." He gives me puppy dog eyes and hangs his head.

I lose my gusto. "Don't do that."

"Do what?" He bats his thick lashes at me. "You know you love me."

"Not like that. It's not fair." My lip quivers as I try not to smile.

"Say it. Say iiihhht." He nudges me.

"Fine, I'll go along with it, but you need to promise we'll tell your mom later that it won't work out. Better yet, I'll tell her I found you cheating on me with another woman."

Comically, Colin sucks in a breath and presses a hand to his chest. "How scandalous!"

"It'll build your rep as a ladies' man. Your father will love that one. Every senator—or senator's son—needs a good sex scandal."

I'm half kidding, but we need a way out of this. If I agree, we'll be shoved down the aisle with no escape plan. It can't come to that, for both our sakes.

Marrying my best friend is one thing, but skipping the sex and love parts of marriage robs us both—and for what? Because his parents don't know their kid? I understand what a difficult situation this is for him, but this isn't the right solution. We need to buy more time.

CHAPTER 24

As the night progresses, I try my best to act like I'm in love with him, but it's hard to feel convincing. It's especially difficult when he kisses me. Each time I feel like we're telling a lie—a lie made worse by his being such a good kisser. Though he's easy on the eyes and can make my heart pitter patter with his kisses, I can only think of Colin as a friend.

I never considered him like that. How could I when I knew he wasn't into my gender? It's like a class action rejection. I wasn't signing up for that heartache, and somehow I still walked right into the dead zone. I'll die here alone, with no real lover, no real kisses.

I'm screwing us both over by going along with this. I know I am, but it's not my secret to tell, and he is my best friend.

As we dance, I glance around the room at the other couples, wondering how many of the relationships are fake. When my eyes land on Jane and Cameron, a spark of hope flickers within me. Seeing them together is like watching a romance movie come to life. He rests his hand against her cheek, her hazel eyes gazing up at him with intense longing. Then she leans into his hand, closing her eyes as his thumb strokes her cheek. He ducks his head to place his lips softly onto hers, and I can't help but gape at them, wishing I were lucky enough to have someone think I hold the stars in place.

I smile sadly, and I know Colin can feel it. He knows me too well. "It's not forever, Beth."

"It was supposed to be..." my voice is a whisper, and the hollow spot in the center of my chest feels like it's going to crush me.

"I know. Beth, I can't thank you enough for this. I know what it means for you." Colin whispers into my ear.

He spins me around, and I see Michael Frey surrounded by a group of people including a few influential senators. Catherine and Anne Degatto stand directly to his right, and my mother stands to his left, uncharacteristically silent and hanging on his every word.

Mr. Frey is the only one not wearing a mask. He looks the same as I remember him. His thick wavy hair is dark with distinguished streaks of gray shooting through it at the temples. His skin is lightly tanned from the Texas sun. Catherine Degatto says something to him, and he gives her one of those smiles politicians always wear, revealing white teeth that are either trustworthy or predatory, depending on the camera angle. After a moment, he gazes in Colin's direction and tilts his head slightly, motioning him over.

The music stops, and Colin sighs. "Let's get this over with and greet the old man before I turn into a pumpkin. Come on."

"I don't think I can do this, Colin." Colin's father is intimidating, and I'm already emotionally unsteady. "He'll see right through this, and my mother's standing beside him."

Colin glances at them and then squeezes my hand. "He won't say anything. Tonight is too important for him."

"Mr. Frey." A familiar deep voice interrupts from behind us. "If you don't mind, I'd like the pleasure of dancing with Miss Bennet."

A dark-haired man in a black mask circles from behind to step between Mr. Frey's groupies and us. Even in four-inch heels, this hot stranger is an inch or two taller than me and oozing sex appeal. I can't help but drink in his incredibly broad shoulders. His tux fits snug against his muscular body. The curve of his mask highlights his sexy lips and the smattering of dark stubble along his chiseled face.

My heart skips a beat as he studies me beneath thick, dark lashes. The royal blue lining of his mask matches his bright eyes. Our eyes lock and his lips curl into a delicious smirk. My stomach flitters as I realize who this man is.

"Of course, Mr. Darcy. I'm sure Beth would love to," Colin holds out my hand, offering it to him. "I have business to attend to elsewhere."

I panic, unable to come up with an excuse. Use your words, Beth! Damn it, say no!

"Have fun," Colin whispers in my ear as he kisses my cheek, "and close your mouth. Gaping isn't attractive."

I shut my mouth and frown as I watch Colin leave. There's a sound of violins as the orchestra starts playing again.

"Do you know the tango, Miss Bennet?"

I gaze down at William's open hand and then back up into ocean blue eyes. Other women fall over themselves wanting to have his hands on their skin, to feel his rock hard body pressed against their own, to run their tongue along his jaw...

I did that and more, but it's as if the night by the pool never happened.

It comes rushing back to me now.

Darcy is a beacon, calling to me, tempting me. My hands float up and slide into his warm palms. His fingers wrap around mine gently even though those eyes are thinking about something else entirely. His mouth opens ever so slightly, and his breathing grows shallow. I know he's also thinking about the other night, about where his hands were and how he made me feel. My stomach flips and my body flushes crimson.

"Dance with me." His voice is low and rough. It catches in his throat sounding almost guttural. I wonder what noises he'd make if I touched him the way he touched me. If I slid my hand along his hard length and felt him in my hand, would he groan and toss his head back. Would he say my name?

I'm close to trembling. I haven't had to deal with anything like this publicly before. As he guides me to the center of the dance floor, I realize there are too many eyes. Too many people will see me not with Colin, and I can't hide how enamored I am with William Darcy.

I find my voice, "We shouldn't."

"It's only a dance, Elizabeth." His deep voice sends a current through me, peaking my senses and making me mute. The way he says my name is an aphrodisiac and I want more. I want to hear it again.

"I thought you only referred to me as Miss Bennet?" I smile coyly at him as he slides his hand down my back, and lightly touches the spot just above my hip. It's blatantly improper. What is he thinking?

He dips his head and begins to lead us across the floor. The corner of his mouth tips up into a boyish grin. "I think we're a little more intimate than that, aren't we?"

My face heats up, and I'm sure my skin is the color of my dress. Did he say that? He lifts his arm and leads me through, pulling me back tightly to his chest. His hand returns to the small of my back as his fingers slip down and graze the top of my butt.

There are too many words, thoughts, and emotions colliding together inside my head. I want this. I want a man that excites me. Colin's kisses seem like kittens compared to a mere look from Darcy. The intense gaze of his eyes takes my breath away, and I'm not even mentioning what he does to the rest of me. Tingles shoot up and down my arms, the skin on my legs is begging to be touched, my nipples are taut and straining against my bra, and that last place—the one that matters most when it comes to a man—it's already wet.

When did I become this woman? How am I so aroused by a guy like this? He's nothing I want, but my body says he's everything I need. My mind is at war, and my emotions cast a thick fog over everything. If I marry Colin, I lose this. I forfeit my chance for a fairy tale ending and my first shot at true love. I'll die a martyr for my best friend, and my lady parts will shrivel up in solitude. Real or fake, I'm not cheating once I'm married. It's a promise of loyalty, and I keep my promises.

Darcy presses his cheek to mine. I breathe in slowly, jaggedly, inhaling his scent. It fills my head, making me feel like I could float away from all these problems. I close my eyes, and we dance like that for a moment, or maybe a day, I don't know. It feels too long, so I pull away.

Darcy's hard gaze isn't there when I step back and glance up into his face. In its place is a man who seemingly understands what I'm doing, a man who understands how much Colin means to me. I finally manage, "I'm engaged."

"I know."

I nod once, then again. My eyes stay on the floor, fixed to his shiny black shoes. I hold my hands, wringing them, wishing for something I'm not brave enough to admit I want. "So, this isn't appropriate."

"It was only a dance, unless…" He steps into my face and tucks a finger under my chin. He tips my head back so he can meet my gaze. "Unless you want more."

Darcy watches me, not explaining his meaning, not needing to.

I nod before I can speak.

Suddenly his heels are together like a soldier dismissed. His familiar cold expression slides back over his face, and I'm left wondering what happened. I thought he wanted me? I thought he was asking? I rub my arms to chase away the rising goose bumps and watch his back disappear into the crowd. My stomach sinks as I realize what happened.

Darcy suggested our little infatuation is only a flirtation. We could stop whenever we want. But then I admitted I'd be unfaithful to a man who values loyalty above all else.

What have I done?

CHAPTER 25

I wander out of the ballroom and onto the balcony, needing space to think. After a few minutes, Jane finds me. Her cheeks are pink with excitement, and there's a spring in her step. It's wonderful to see her so happy.

She laughs and hands me a champagne flute. "Beth, tonight has been incredible."

I take a sip and glance over at her. "It has been. I saw you and Cameron together. You two look like you're trapped in a fairytale."

"If that's true, I hope we never have to turn the page." She tips her head back and smiles at the stars. My lovestruck sister never shows this much emotion, ever.

"I'm happy for you, Jane. Truly. You better get back in there, Cameron will be missing you."

She nods, placing her half-empty glass on a nearby table. When she turns back to me, the smile fades from her face. "Are you all right? I saw you dancing with Darcy, and I know you don't care for him. You seemed upset."

I fabricate a smile and hold it in place. I'm not ruining her night with my drama. Plus, I have no idea what I think about any of this. I want to figure that out before I cry on her—because that's what I feel like doing. But I can't. She's filled with joy, and I can't snuff it out.

I roll my eyes and put on the full act. "Jane, I'm fine. He said something dickish, that's all. Between him, Colin, and Mr. Frey—I just needed some air."

"I understand." She places her small hand lightly on my shoulder. "You are beautiful, Beth. No one can make you feel bad about yourself without your permission."

"Stop channeling Eleanor Roosevelt." I tease, giving her arm a gentle push. "Go back to the ball. Enjoy your night with the prince."

Her nose crinkles up, and she giggles. "I know, right?"

"Dance until your feet give out, so Cameron will have to carry you home on his steed."

She blushes and swats at me. "Don't call it that!"

"Jane!" My eyes nearly bug out of my head. She never says anything remotely perverted. We both giggle for a moment before she disappears inside.

I turn to resume my study of the city below. A spattering of stars rarely seen here shine brightly tonight. The lights from Manhattan usually drown them out. I'm lost in thought, looking at the world below, wondering if life could ever be so beautiful, so picturesque, when I feel eyes on my back.

I turn slowly and come face to face with Darcy. He towers above me, no mask, and inclines his head. "I need to speak to you, to ask you something."

"So ask me, then." I swallow hard, expecting to be blindsided with scorn, but Darcy presses his lips together and closes his eyes. He glances past me once, and then reaches for my hand.

"Come with me."

CHAPTER 26

Once inside, he drops my hand, and I follow him to the elevators. I wonder where we're going, but I don't ask. He either wants to chew me out, or throw me off the balcony. I deserve both.

When we step inside, he pushes the button for the penthouse. Tension flows off Darcy in waves. It feels as if we may drown in this small space. I step back to make a buffer between us. His face is dark and his mood is volatile.

I open my mouth, still working out something to say, when the doors slide open. A large group of Japanese businessmen pile into the elevator with us. Darcy slips behind me to make space for them. I don't understand what the men are saying, but one of them holds the elevator door open, motioning the rest of the group to join us—even though there's no more room. The men laugh as they squeeze themselves in. I'm pushed further back into the small cube until I'm pressed tight against Darcy. I bite down on my lip as I feel his hand move to rest low on my hip, fingers grazing my outer thigh. His breath is on my neck, and his lips are close enough to kiss my temple. I step back a fraction of an inch, attempting to avoid being stepped on, and am surprised when I feel more than a toned body and firm hips against my behind. He's hard. What the hell is going on? He comes up here to chew me out and then gets turned on by businessmen?

The doors finally close, and the men talk rapidly, laughing. All I can think about is the heat of his body and his hot breath whispering over my bare shoulder. His hand moves away from my hip and leaves a cold spot in its wake.

What am I doing? Colin will be disappointed if he thinks I've left. I'm supposed to talk with Mr. Frey. I'm supposed to be convincing. Getting into this elevator was piss-poor judgment on my part. I vowed nothing would ever happen between me and William Darcy again, but right now my mind is drawing Mrs. Elizabeth Darcy surrounded by little hearts all over my brain—even though I'm here to receive a verbal lashing for being me.

For being unfaithful.

For wanting Darcy.

For wishing Colin would just tell his parents the truth.

The elevator numbers light up as we pass each floor. No one gets off. Crap. It's way past warm in here. A bead of sweat rolls down my back and, with the way this dress is cut, I'm sure Darcy can see it.

I feel a light brush of skin against my thigh, and I stiffen, thinking the businessman next to me is feeling me up. Darcy's rich voice whispers, "Relax."

My breath hitches when he slips a hand into the slit of my gown. My body bursts into flames when he begins to stroke my thigh. I want to throw my head back and moan with each caress. Instead, my eyes fixate on the numbers.

Twelve. Thirteen.

He gently squeezes my ass leaving his hand to linger, to caress. I stare at the numbers, willing myself to be silent, to not moan and melt into him. Does he want to be with me? What the hell is he doing?

Fourteen. Fifteen.

That warm hand travels to the front, agonizingly slow, sweeping over the outside of my lace panties. My stomach twists as my breath hitches and my heart pounds harder.

Sixteen. Seventeen.

Fingers brush over the thin lace barrier, once, then twice. My chest tightens as I force air into my lungs. I stand rigid, unable to turn and face him. Part of me wants to slap him. The other part wants things I can't have.

Eighteen. Nineteen.

He's moving a single finger in smooth circles. A delicious sensation is building inside me. Things are hot, wet, and breathless. My mind is racing, trying to rationalize this occurrence. Did he plan this? Did Darcy hire out a truckload of guys to press me against his... Oh My. God. He thrusts his hips against my back, and I want to turn toward him, but he holds me in place.

Blinking rapidly, I look up, face flushed, breathing jagged. The doors slide open.

Twenty.

Darcy moves quickly, cutting through the crowd of people. He places a hand on the small of my back, leading me from behind, pushing me into the hallway. Before I can say anything, his touch changes from gentle to rough. He practically shoves me to a nearby exit and into the stairwell.

"Watch your step." That voice, the way it slides out of his mouth. I swear he could command me to come right now and I would. The way he speaks is liquid sex, hot and smooth, caressing me in all the right places.

I climb a flight of stairs, feeling his hot gaze on my ass watching it shift in this tight red dress. The material slips over my curves with each step, and the little train pools behind me as I climb.

He pushes us through a metal door, and we're outside. A rush of wind blows my hair off my shoulders. The moon and stars provide the only light up here. I look out at the city far below. It's my city, my home. I've missed this place, everything from the smell of the air to the sounds that make New York unique. There's one other thing that makes this city breathtaking, and he's standing behind me.

I don't know what to say. I have no idea what he wants, but he seems so torn. The way his brow wrinkles and those eyes narrow to slits, I'd think he was going to scream at me. He's angry, upset with himself and with me. I shouldn't have said that downstairs. I should have acted cold and unconcerned. I could have continued to pretend I hate him, but when I saw him tonight something inside me changed. I don't want him to hate himself every time he sees me. I need to explain, that was my fault—the pool, the kiss, and the other stuff.

I suck in a generous amount of night air and leave my mouth hanging open for too long. My hands lift, and I shake my head. "William? William, I—"

I called him by his first name. After he called me by mine, I had to—it felt right. But now, when he lifts his gaze to meet mine, I shrink back. Rage mixes with fire and ignites within him. I see it explode in those brilliantly beautiful eyes.

With a sudden fierceness, he steps toward me, grabs me by the waist, jerks me to him, and silences me when he crushes his mouth to mine. Those lips—those hot, perfectly swollen, soft lips—ravage mine, making me feel faint. His stubble rubs against my chin as he does so, leaving it raw. His tongue slips between the seams of my lips and deepens the kiss instantly, demanding more.

The scent of him is all around me. I'm drowning in his touch, his scent, and his taste. We're moving back, and I'm against a cold brick wall. I shriek into his mouth as my spine curves away from the brick, pushing harder against his chest. Darcy moans into my mouth as his fingers stretch across my cheeks, cradling my face.

My pulse pounds deafeningly in my ears as my stomach fills with butterflies. Waves of emotion batter against me from within, warring, each wanting to win. Darcy is going to hate himself for this. Pull away. Then the feel of his lips on mine cuts through the thought and I've lost the string. I can't remember what I was thinking, and my hands tangle in his hair as I lift a knee up along his thigh.

Desperate to feel his hard body beneath my fingertips, I slide my hands under his jacket, looking for the hem of his shirt. I want to feel those hot muscles under my hands. I want to do things to him, things I never understood before, things I'd deny in the light of day.

In an instant, his jacket is off. And my hands fly down his shirt, almost ripping off his buttons. When my hand touches his hot, muscled stomach, I moan with pleasure.

I tug at his shirt, lifting it, crawling it up out of his pants. He's breathing heavily, watching me as I unbutton his tux shirt. My thoughts won't leave this alone. I need to feel the pads of my fingers slide across his tight nipples. I want to lean in and press my face to his chest and lick the lines of his abs down to his waist, down to his…

My lips are suddenly there, unapologetic and unmasking. I press my mouth against his hard chest over and over again, working my way to the part I want. Those dark little buds of flesh stand up for me. I wrap my lips around one and flick it with my tongue. Darcy shudders and his hand moves over my back, unzipping my gown. I inhale deeply as the constricting pressure of the bodice loosens.

I'm afraid to look into his eyes, afraid of what I'll see there, so I keep my head lowered and my eyes on his chest. I wrap my arms around his back and dig my fingernails into his soft skin, as my lips travel down his chest. I want to go lower, kneel, and do more. I never, in my life, have wanted to do this—

but now I can't stop. I want his dick in my mouth so I can taste him, feel him, suck him until he says my name.

But Darcy has other plans. He takes me by the shoulders and presses me back into the wall with one strong arm across my chest. My gown is barely hanging on and slips down one shoulder, revealing bare skin and a tight nipple. Darcy's lips part, forming an O, as he leans in toward me. It's agonizing waiting for his lips to touch me, but he doesn't go directly to my breast, he starts higher, at my neck.

Darcy works his way down, holding me in place as he does so. When he reaches the tops of my breasts, he releases me and shoves the bodice down. Both breasts are exposed, rising and falling softly as I breathe.

He watches me for a moment, his eyes seeing nothing but my curves before he wets his lips and bows his head. I suck in air and press back into the wall as Darcy takes my breast in his mouth. He gently flicks my nipple with his tongue, pressing it with his teeth, and then sucking gently while he slips his mouth away.

I can't breathe. I can't cry out. There's no air, no words. I close my eyes and arch my back, aching for more. Then he's there, his face alongside my breast, sweeping his cheek against my soft skin. His stubble prickles, scratching me, filling me with pleasure and pain. I gasp and nearly cry out when his mouth returns to my chest and takes in my nipple, sucking it hard, nipping me with his teeth.

I whimper as his stubbled chin scrapes along my breasts, alternating from one nipple to the other. I tangle my hands in his hair, wanting to guide him, but he pins my hands to the wall and crushes his body to mine. His mouth is on mine, and the kiss heats me, making my core pulse softly as I imagine him inside me.

I wrap a leg around him, needing him against me. He lifts me and presses me against the wall, allowing me to straddle him. When I lock my heels around his waist, Darcy tips his head back and closes his eyes for a moment. His jaw drops, and he makes a sound I want to hear again. It's raw, filled with pleasure. He's normally so guarded, so in control of himself. To see Darcy like this, lost in passion, it's unthinkable. It feels like magic, like a fairytale.

The thought jars the conversation I had with Jane earlier, about her fairytale. This is something else, and I'm drowning in the moment. This isn't real. This isn't him, and it's not me.

"William." I say his name once, and the amount of control in my voice shocks me.

He looks up, a sheen of sweat on the brow of his beautiful face. I'm breathing hard, looking into his eyes, and he knows. He puts me down, and I straighten my gown, zipping it closed.

Darcy stands there, white shirt in stark contrast against the inky night sky, chest bared and his jacket in a puddle of cloth on the ground. He breathes in, and I watch his pecs swell until he releases the air and repeats.

"I wish…" I stammer trying to find words, but there are none. I watch him with remorse, knowing there can't ever be anything between us. I've chosen my path, and Darcy knows his. They don't meet. There's no intersection. We can't do this.

I don't have to say more. He read it in my eyes before I said his name. I expect him to go cold again and shun me, but he doesn't. Instead, he stands there, hands in his pockets, looking like a god with that perfect body.

"I know. So do I."

I tuck my chin and avoid his gaze, meaning to walk past him to the door. Darcy reaches out and takes my arm. I look down at his hand and then up into his face. "This was never meant to be, you know that as well as I do."

Darcy blinks slowly, parting his lips to speak, but nothing comes out. Instead, he drops his hand and stands aside, shoving his hand back into his pocket. He's letting me leave.

I'm at the door, the cold metal knob is in my hand, but I'm frozen, unable to leave. Glancing over my shoulder, I say softly, "I should have said no. You're not this guy, and I can't bear for you to hate yourself because of me."

Darcy looks away as if I slapped him. His tone is sharp when he speaks. "You think too highly of yourself, Miss Bennett. One loose woman doesn't make a difference to me." He smiles and turns away, not seeing how his words rip my heart in two.

————

I don't sleep that night. Jane is high from her date with Cameron, giggling about him until she passes out close to dawn. I'm tired of lying here, and I've had way too much time to think about Darcy. I need to banish him from my mind, so I drag my body out of bed and pull on sweats. After strapping my sneakers to my feet, I'm out the door, headed to the park.

As I pad down the hall, I hear an odd noise coming from Mary's room. It's almost a cooing sound. I smile. Mary tried to free Lucy over ten times, but Lucy keeps coming back.

Soon I'm outside and jogging into the park. The city is covered with a thin layer of fog this morning.

As I hit the trail in the park, I watch the sun rise between the trees. Orange and gold streak through the sky and begin to burn off the haze.

By the time I'm ready to fall over, I've run over five miles and still have to get home. I slow and let my pulse come back down. My goal was to run until I no longer thought of Darcy, but my mind is never far from him. I don't know how he can be so cold and cruel after something like that.

I was nothing to him, a conquest. I got it. I don't need another humiliating lesson in love with William Darcy to figure it out. But still, for a moment, I believed him, and I guess that's the problem.

CHAPTER 27

"Excuse me. I need to get to the sugar packets."
I look up at the young woman holding a carrier with
cups of coffee.

"Oh, sorry about that." I move out of her way.
It's crowded in the coffeehouse, people sipping hot
beverages as they stare robotically at laptops and cell
phones. Baristas yell out orders, competing with the
low rumble of the crowd and the anchorwoman
reading out the morning news from the wall-
mounted corner television.

After not sleeping last night, I'm in desperate
need of caffeine. Waking up at four in the morning
every day for the past few weeks to accompany Dad
to his office has been a challenge. I'm not sure how
much help I am to him. Instead of getting better, he
seems to be getting worse. I keep busy doing as
much as he allows me to do. A few days, he even left
the office early to rest while I stayed and finished up

some paperwork for him. At least, I thought he went home to rest. Sometimes he'd leave in the afternoon, but when I finally got home late in the evening, he wasn't at the apartment. Then there were times he'd leave in the middle of the afternoon for hours at a time. At first, I thought he was just at a business meeting, but when even his receptionist didn't know where he was, I grew suspicious. I'd text his phone, but he wouldn't respond. I tried to talk with him about it, but he'd wave me away saying his work was confidential.

By the time I got home from my run this morning, Dad had already left without me. He wrote a note telling me to take my time and requested I pick up a cappuccino for him on my way.

"Grande cappuccino, tall hazelnut latte, and tall mocha," a voice calls out.

I take my drinks and am making my way through the crowd when I hear a familiar name through the television's speakers.

"And in business news, Marcia Davis, CFO of the multi-billion dollar corporation Darcy Biopharm, has taken on a new role as head of the newly formed Darcy Foundation."

My jaw drops as William's face appears on the screen. He speaks into a reporter's microphone. "Darcy Biopharm's loss is our foundation's gain. I can think of no other person with Ms. Davis' skills better suited to nurture and grow the Darcy Foundation. Through her leadership, the Foundation will help the lives of millions suffering from preventable diseases in third world countries."

The camera pans to an attractive woman with curly black hair and caramel skin. "This is a great honor. My coworkers at Darcy Biopharm are like family to me, and though I'll miss them all, I'm happy to continue my connection with Darcy Biopharm through my work with the Darcy Foundation. Furthermore, I'm thrilled to have the opportunity to positively affect the lives of so many people. I would never have had such a wonderful opportunity without the generosity and guidance of William Darcy."

Darcy's face is still commanding the news channels when I arrive at Dad's office suite. I glare at the TV. He's still an asshat.

"Hi, Sandra," I say to Dad's secretary, pausing at her desk. "I got you a mocha."

"Thanks, Beth." She smiles as I hand her the drink.

There wasn't an extra room in the suite, so Dad placed my desk next to Sandra's. You can't really call it a desk, more a folding table and chair with a laptop. Dad offered to buy office furniture for me, but spending more money was the last thing I wanted him to do.

Still lost in my thoughts, I enter Dad's office with his coffee. It's empty. I turn back to Sandra. "Where's my father? Is he at a business meeting?"

She glances at her computer. "He has something marked on his calendar, but it's set to private. Would you like me to call him for you?"

"No, thanks." I open my laptop and tackle the stack of paper on my desk. My tasks are monotonous and boring, so I alternate between checking Facebook and doing work.

A few hours pass with no sign of dad. I'm thinking of sending him a text when I get a Facebook message from Jane.

JANE: Are you busy?
ME: No. What's up?
JANE: Cameron broke up with me.
ME: What? Are you sure?
JANE: We're supposed to go to a B&B in Vermont tomorrow. He canceled. He said he had to leave for San Jose and didn't know when he'd be back.
ME: Maybe he's just going away on business?
JANE: No. He broke up with me. It's over.

My Facebook page refreshes and I see Jane's status. She's listening to Adele, which means she's crying her ass off.

ME: Awh, Jane. Don't worry. It's just a *business trip. He'll be back.*

JANE: *I don't think so. It's like he broke up with me without breaking up with me.*

ME: *Are you sure?*

JANE: *He texted that he was canceling. He won't return my calls.*

ME: *That could mean anything. It's not you, Jane. Maybe he…*

Before I can finish, her next message appears.

JANE: *He deleted his Facebook page.*

Quickly, I scroll through my list of Facebook friends and click on an icon of Cameron's smiling face. Nothing. Shit. This can't be right. He loves her!

JANE: *I don't know what to do. I love him, Beth.*

I close my eyes, fighting back pain I feel on Jane's behalf. Out of all of us, she most deserves to be happy and cherished. Something bad must've happened. I eye Gwen's photo on my list of Facebook friends. She would know what's going on.

I'm about to send her a message when the office door opens, followed by Sandra's gasp.

"Mr. Darcy!" Sandra's hands fly up to her messy hair, smoothing it. "It's an honor to meet you, sir. Mr. Bennet isn't in at the moment. I didn't realize he had an appointment with you this morning."

Sandra is flustered as Dickwad approaches her desk. Even when he's wearing his don't-bother-me expression, he's amazingly attractive. But today, he's different. The perpetual brooding look on his face is gone. His dark hair is tousled as if he's been running his hands through it nervously. His eyes are warm and incredibly blue. His face is completely open, relaxed, and vulnerable, reminding me of the expression Cameron wears every time I see him with Jane.

My stomach sours immediately. I study him suspiciously and notice he's dressed casually, too casually for someone like him and in the middle of the workweek. He's wearing dark gray slacks and a white, collared shirt that highlights his handsome face.

He lifts his eyes and startles when they lock on mine. I suck in my breath at the raw emotion on his face. My mind flashes over our last encounter—the taste of his mouth, his skin, his hands all over my body—followed up by the message every woman wants to receive: You mean nothing to me.

"I don't." His eyes hold mine as he answers Sandra. "I was hoping to drop in and catch him for a moment. It's all right. I'll try again another time."

Darcy is staring at me as if he wants to say something else, but he doesn't. Sandra throws a quick look at me and then back to Darcy. The room grows still for a moment. I'm too busy willing my heart to stop slamming into my ribs to wonder why he's looking for Dad.

Sandra finally cuts the tension, and visibly startles Darcy. "Would you like some coffee?"

"No, thank you." He's still staring at me.

What the fuck? Just go away. Pretend last night never happened. Don't come back and look at me like I'm a freak later.

"Move along Darcy. All your conquests, I mean concerns, have been added to Dad's notes. You want me to tell him anything else?" Like how you defiled his daughter on the roof of a hotel and then acted like she was trash?

I blink at him, ready to verbally bitchslap him. Goddamnit! Say something. Why doesn't he move? He just stands there in front of my desk, looking at me.

"Grow a pair, Darcy. If you have something to say, spit it out." I tap my nails on the desk and glare up at him.

His eyes dart around the office as he wipes his hands nervously on his slacks.

Sandra starts laughing nervously, which seems to snap him out of it. Darcy turns to her and nods once in a courteous way. "I'm sorry to have bothered you."

"It was no bother. Stop by anytime." Sandra walks him out the door, and when she reappears a moment later, she's visibly flushed. "Beth! The way you spoke! Do you know him?"

"Not very well, it would seem."

Sandra smiles broadly at me in an unreal way, leaving her jaw dropped too long, obviously excited. "Can you imagine? THE William Darcy! Here? In this office? I wonder what that was all about!"

"A mistake," I whisper to myself. "An incredibly huge mistake."

CHAPTER 28

The rest of the morning crawls by like an unending funeral procession. I'm holding my head up with my hand, and my elbow's gone numb from sitting too long.

Colin bounces through the door. "Oh, thank goodness. You're here," he says out of breath. "I have to talk to you."

Sandra glances my way. "Should I scan some more files?" That's code for, 'do you need privacy?'

"No, but thanks for offering. We'll go into Dad's office."

"Bring your laptop with you," Colin shouts as he struts into the little room. When I close the door to Dad's office, Colin plops on the loveseat, grinning at me. He folds his hands in his lap and looks like he ate the cat and the canary. "So."

"So what?" I'm grumpy. Today sucked. Yesterday sucked. I'm on the train to Suck Town and can't seem to get off.

"Don't play coy with me. I know you have a thing with Darcy."

"What?" My voice raises an octave as I whirl around and stare at him. "I do not!"

He blinks and makes a face. "Ok. Someone needs new PMS pills. I meant, what'd you do to Darcy? I ran into him earlier, and he looked like he might throw up. He came from here, so I naturally assumed it was you."

"Gee, thanks." My mouth grows dry. I grab a small watering can and busy myself watering the plants. "Did he say something?"

"No. He didn't notice me."

I let out a breath. "No clue."

"I'm surprised he's leaving with all his body parts after what he did. I'm surprised he had the balls to come here at all. Why was he here?"

I pinch dead leaves off one of the office plants, buying time. If I turn around, Colin will see it on my face—I did too much with Darcy, and now I regret it. Turns out his manners only apply to pleases and thank yous. They have little to do with nailing yours truly on a roof.

Plus, Colin will run Darcy over with his Hummer if he thinks I'm hurt and, since I want him thinking that I don't care, Colin can't know about it.

"He wanted to meet with Dad about some business stuff. Nothing important. He ran in and ran out, managing to get his oversized asshat caught in the door. It was a sight to see." I set down the watering can, tip my head to the side and smile placidly. "Fun times."

Colin smirks. "OMG! You don't know."

Colin's eyes are huge, and he's pressing his fingertips together. I laugh deeply and shake my head, careful to make eye contact, but not for long enough that he can really look at me. "So, what'd Asshat do?"

Please don't say, 'he did you.' Please, please, please!

"Seriously, you don't know? Anne Degatto said Darcy saved Cameron from making a huge mistake. He was going to ask Jane to marry him."

"Wait, slow down. What do you mean Darcy 'saved' Cameron?"

"That's what I'm trying to tell you." He's talking with his hands now, trying to get my full attention. "Darcy convinced Cameron to break up with Jane."

"He did not."

"He did. But it gets better! Cameron didn't want to hurt Jane." Colin's like a cat batting a mouse when he has juicy gossip. Just say it already!

"Colin, what did he do?" My voice is a low monotone. I glare at him.

He flinches. "Holy shit, Bethy-pie. You're channeling a little too much of your mom there. Dial it back down."

"TELL ME!"

"Okay, okay! Darcy told Cameron he needed to end things, and if he didn't want to be cruel, he could gradually disappear from her life—slip away like a boat that someone forgot to tie up. Like a dog with no leash. Like a—"

"Like a foot up your ass." I smile at him, fluttering my eyes like a 50's housewife.

"You're cranky today. Fine, long story short, he told Cameron to go to San Jose on an extended business trip, and that over time Jane would forget about him and move on to someone else."

I blink at him, stunned. Why would someone do that to Jane and Cameron? Anyone can see they are in love. Darcy broke them up. It comes to me slowly, contorting my face in stages until I erupt. "Holy fuck! Who does he think he is? Darcy can't make them not love each other."

Dial it down, Beth! He'll figure out that something else is going on. Colin's not an idiot. He's watching me with his beady little hawk eyes right now. I throw my head back and strangle the air. "She was so happy, Colin. Now she's devastated! I talked to her earlier, and she says she'll be fine, but damn! Why can't people stay out of other people's business?" I sit down hard next to him.

Colin practically bounces in the air before settling back into his slouchy spot. "Yeah, you're preaching to the choir, girl. Have you met my parents?"

"What now?" I rush ahead, thinking he might have told them the truth. "Did you come out and them you're gay? What did they say?"

"No, I didn't. But if I don't do something soon to fix this, I'm dead," he groans and covers his face with his arm.

"They're not going to kill you, Colin. Your parents love you even if they have a funny way of showing it."

He opens up my laptop and starts typing. "Uh, yeah. You'll change your mind after you see this." After a few clicks, he hands it to me. "Take a look."

"You're overreacting." The screen is open to the Ruben Micucci website, an extremely popular web blog for celebrity news and gossip. "There's nothing you can show me that—Damn, Colin! What are you wearing? Are those leather chaps?"

He juts out his jaw. "Yup."

"Um, aren't you supposed to wear something underneath them, like oh, I don't know, clothes? This is clearly not a commando outfit! Why is your ass on this website?"

"Yeah, that'd be why my parents are going to kill me." He looks at me sheepishly.

I gawk at the photo, shaking my head. For such a smart guy, Colin does stupid things sometimes. The blurry picture is of a crowd of people hanging around outside a well-known gay bar. Mateo is in the mix, shirtless, wearing skintight leather pants. He's standing close to a man wearing black leather chaps, clearly groping that man's bare ass.

"Maybe no one will notice," I offer hopefully. "Your face is hidden."

"You knew it was me!"

"Only because you're wearing the neon green cowboy boots I bought you for your birthday last year."

"Did you read the blurb? Micucci names me as one of the people in the picture. It's only a matter of time before the mainstream media picks up on it. Please, Beth, you have to help me out of this."

My eyes skim over the blurb. It mentions Colin as the son of Michael Frey and speculates whether Colin's sexual orientation will be a factor in his father's run for Senate in Texas. "I don't know what

I can do to help. Maybe we could email Micucci and ask him to take it down."

"Please. Micucci would never do that. Look how many comments the post has. It barely went up an hour ago!" Colin sounds frantic. I scroll through the comments. There are over a thousand of them.

"That's not good. But look at the bright side. A lot of the comments are very supportive. This one says he's behind you all the way when you decide to come out. Hey!"

Colin slams the lid shut, barely missing my fingers. "You CAN help me, Beth. Marry me." He places a black box onto the laptop. "Now."

"What? Today?" I laugh at him. "That's not going to make this go away. It's a Band-Aid. You can't hide who you are—obviously, considering your naked ass is plastered across a gossip blog—no matter how much you want to protect your parents. Even if you do marry me, people are going to talk about this."

"I know you're right, but it buys me time. Deep inside, I always knew my parents saw me as their trophy boy. Someone to show off as the future heir to their oil empire." His voice sounds harsh as he speaks, shoving his hands into his hair and tugging hard. He sighs and sinks back into the couch, tucking his chin to his chest, afraid to look up at me.

"Why do you put up with it? Why would you live a lie for this?"

Glistening eyes meet mine. "They're the only family I have."

My heart aches for him. It's not true. "You're wrong, Colin." I reach for the box. "I'm your family, too." Taking the ring out, I slide it onto my ring finger on my left hand. I hold my hand out, wiggling my fingers. "I always have been and always will be. If a piece of paper makes your life that much better, I can't say no."

His face turns serious as if he can't believe that I'm doing this. "I'm sorry. I understand how much I'm asking of you."

I take his hand. "Yes, I am sure. You've saved me from enough heartache and disasters. It seems silly to wait around for a fantasy."

"Beth," he shakes his head and tries to take the ring off my finger.

"Hey!" I pull my hand away. "No backsies. It's mine. Back off bitch!"

Colin offers a weak smile. He knows I'm fucking up my life to cover this up. Making light of it brings out the best in him, the guy that wants me to be happy.

"You're really going to go through with this?"

"Are you really going to walk down the aisle with me? Do you really want to live with me? I'm kind of a pain in the ass. Ask my mother."

He laughs. "No, you're not. You're selfless and perfect, beautiful inside and out. I couldn't dream up a better person." He wraps his arms around me and kisses my cheek. Tears prickle my eyes, but I blink them back.

I know how much shit he's taken, just from the gossip that he might be gay. Being rich, Texan, and a politician's son leaves no room for the truth. They'll beat it out of him if I don't help, and the friend I love will wither away. This will protect him. It's something I can do.

We both swat away tears when we pull back. I stand and hold out my hand in the light. "Now, for the worst part."

"Which is…?"

"We have to tell Mother."

I open my Facebook page and click on Relationship Status. I click on the arrow button and moved from Single to Engaged. Slowly, I type in the name: Colin Frey.

CHAPTER 29

I focus on the rhythm of my feet slapping against the pavement, the whoosh of air and accompanying flap of my t-shirt as my arms pump in an opposite motion. White clouds of mist pass over my lips and into the path before me as my lungs pant warm breath into the crisp evening air. The sun touches the tops of the trees, casting long, playful shadows as it descends. I wind and weave down the familiar trail through Central Park for the second time in twenty-four hours. Drowning my sorrows in jogging is better than drowning my sorrows in ice cream, right?

I left as late as I could from the office, dreading the thought of facing my mother. After my Facebook post, Mrs. Frey took the matter of publicity into her own hands. The official announcement of our engagement went viral before dinnertime. By bedtime, we were trending on Twitter.

'Meet the future Frey,' headlines on every conceivable society column, followed by a picture of my smiling face and our official wedding date: Valentine's Day. The event will be sooner rather than later.

My life is a lie.

My soon-to-be-husband is gay.

I've still got William Darcy touching me in my dreams. How will I explain that to Colin on our honeymoon? 'Sorry I was moaning in bed last night and woke up all hot and bothered. Dream Darcy was doing me again.' Yeah, perfect.

Dad's spent the afternoon acting all cloak and dagger. He appeared at work after lunch with no explanation for his absence. He was still working at his desk after Sandra had gone home and I'd closed everything else up for the night. I wanted to stay with him, but he insisted I leave. He'd already gotten several emails from business associates congratulating him on my engagement to Colin, and insisted I had "more important things to do than babysit an old man."

The moment I stepped foot into the apartment, Mother began complaining non-stop about Andrea Frey usurping the arrangements. I tried to convince her she could co-host the wedding. Somehow that upset her more than not hosting at all. I should've known better. Mother is all about appearances and allowing Mrs. Frey to hijack the wedding implies we can't afford it—at least, it does in Mother's eyes.

After failing at comforting my mother, I try comforting Jane instead. It hurts my heart to see her eyes red-rimmed and her nose puffy. She put on a brave face as she listened to Mother's plans for our wedding wardrobe, but her heart wasn't in it. Mother was visibly disappointed Cameron was gone, babbling on and on about how Jane should have changed her personality more to Mr. Bingham's preference. She should have been more sociable, more outgoing, more fun, less Jane. When Mother suggested Jane should join a Toastmaster's International club, I just about blew it.

Mother made it sound like it was Jane's fault Cameron left. The way I see it, if Cameron allows Darcy to dictate his life on matters of this importance, he's a moron unworthy of Jane. Either way, that's when I decided I needed to get out of the house.

I force my thoughts to the present, running faster, releasing pent up anger. I'm angry with Mother for failing to see genuine beauty in the daughter she treats like a toy. I'm angry with Dad for allowing both his health and his bank account to deteriorate. I'm angry with Michael and Andrea Frey for not seeing or appreciating the wonderful son they have. Most of all, though, I'm angry with

William Darcy for making me believe there was a decent human being somewhere deep inside him.

I slow down as I near Bethesda Terrace. It's my favorite spot in Central Park. Overlooking the lake from the terrace and hearing the sound of the fountain brings me a sense of peace. I stop running and catch my breath, letting the silence surround me.

Just as my heart rate begins to slow, my phone vibrates intrusively from my pocket startling me and setting me back on edge. Angry all over again, I pull out the phone to read the text message.

MOM: Call me immediately.

I sigh as I return the phone to my pocket. I glance around the terrace, noticing a small group of tourists studying a map and a young couple straddled across matching bikes, drinking water. I place my hands on my hips, walking toward the stone railing, taking in gulps of air. Sweat beads on my forehead and my tank top clings to my body.

Taking a swig of water, I watch the group of tourists leave the terrace, heading off toward their destination. I cough, nearly choking, when I see William Darcy leaning against the stone railing.

My heart races at the sight of him. He's wearing the same white shirt and gray slacks. Except now his face is dark with a five o'clock shadow. His eyes look bloodshot as if he's been crying or drinking. He looks dangerous.

When his eyes lock with mine, I take a step back. There's a fierce determination on his face making his eyes blaze with a brilliant blue fire. I mentally slap myself for being intimidated. He's an asshole of the worst kind.

Jutting my chin out, I snap, "You have some nerve coming here. How the hell did you find me?"

"If you don't want people to know where you are, stop posting your location on Facebook."

"Fuck you."

"I tried, remember?" The corner of his mouth tips up, mirth mingling with that fire boiling beneath the surface.

My eyes flash up when I hear his low chuckle. "I don't need this shit." As I turn to leave, Darcy grabs my arm.

"Wait. There's something I need to say." He pulls me to him. He's so close, I smell the alcohol on his breath. His face changes and the raw emotion I saw earlier is back again.

"What?" I push him away and step back, folding my arms over my chest, waiting.

He takes a breath then his hand is suddenly caressing my face. My eyes widen with shock.

"Beth, I can't stop thinking about you. These past few months have been torturous. I can't eat. I can't sleep. Your face, your words haunt my dreams. I don't understand it."

My eyes narrow and I shake off his hand. He's conning me. He's trying to make me think he's into me. "I fell for this once already. I'm not taking the bait a second time."

He nods slowly. "There were rumors of your engagement to Colin Frey. I didn't want to believe it. You had no ring." He glances at my hand and the huge ass rock on my finger.

"I told you it was true." I wave it in the air at him, wiggling my fingers to show it off.

"I know, but I'd hoped—" he shakes his head and avoids my gaze. "I hoped I wasn't too late, that I could pull you away from him. I had to try."

"I don't understand."

He closes the space between us, cupping his hands on my cheeks, his blue eyes gazing intently into mine. "I want you"—he swallows thickly—"desperately."

It feels like he kicked me in the stomach. I can't breathe. He likes me? No, it's more than that. He's saying he's in love with me? That can't be right. My lips part and my jaw falls open. I can't find the words to convey what I mean, what I feel.

"This is cruel, even coming from you." My hands ball into fists at my sides as tears overflow and spill down my cheeks. "How could you?"

"Beth, please. Give me a chance. It's not too late, not yet. Then I saw the wedding date, and…"

"Stop! You can't do this to me. You can't tell me you want me because some other guy swept me up. I'm marrying Colin, Darcy. Deal with it."

"You're rejecting me then." He looks devastated.

"The conquest is all about the chase, right? I mean, imagine the thrill of bedding me when I was about to walk down the aisle. Imagine me, tossing aside another man for you. You're a prick, and you only think with your dick."

He swallows hard. "You think my feelings are only sexual?"

"There's no reason to lie anymore. I know how you feel."

His eyes widen, and he sounds flustered. "No, you don't. Beth, I love you."

It's like a knife in my heart. I didn't realize it until then, but I wanted to hear him say it. That's the one thing I wanted him to tell me, and I wish it were true.

"Don't lie to me."

"I'm not." His blue eyes bore a hole into my soul. I'm shivering on the spot, part rage, part regret, wishing he were the man I hoped he was. "Despite your upbringing, your vocation, your parents, and even your sisters, I have fallen for you. Everything within me told me to stay away, that you and your kind were nothing but gold diggers, but I can't manage this existence any longer. I need you, Beth."

"Do you really think so little of me?" I laugh and glance around, and then shove him. "You think I'm after your money? Fuck you!" I shove him again. He steps back, indignant.

"Beth—"

"You think I could love someone as heartless and cold as you are? Did you think I wouldn't find out? I know what you did to Jane. It broke her heart! Don't deny it."

"I don't." His deep voice is stern.

A flash of electricity fills the sky behind him followed by a low rumble. The smell of rain fills the air. My temper flares white-hot as the lightning. "Why would you do that to her? Why would you do that to your best friend?" I shove him twice, pushing him back to the wall.

He grabs my wrists and hisses in my face, "Because Cameron is my best friend. He's trusting, fully convinced all people are inherently good. Real life isn't like that, and too many people already take advantage of his kindness."

"Are you suggesting Jane was one of those people?"

His jaw tightens, and his face grows dark. "It's not a suggestion. It's a fact. Just as it's a fact that your father's company will soon be bankrupt, so your mother and Jane colluded to trap Cameron into a marriage that will save your family from financial ruin. It's a fact Jane's not in love with Cameron and a fact Cameron's so blinded by love, he's willing to forego drawing up a prenuptial contract—despite urgings from both his financial advisors and his best friend."

Almost before the words reach my ears, my hand is flying through the air toward his face. Thunder cracks as I simultaneously scream, "You don't know her! How can you speak so absolutely? How could you be so sure that you'd risk ruining both their lives? Your pride blinds you, William Darcy."

He has the audacity to be shocked. "I can understand why you'd defend her. She is your sister after all," he says, rubbing his cheek. "It's unfortunate you're blinded by your love for her."

Screw guilt! My hand flies up ready to strike his cheek a second time. He catches my fist and growls, "Don't."

I jerk my hand out of his. "Who are you to pass judgment against a person you hardly know?"

"I'm not the prejudiced person in this situation."

Tears are streaking down my face, mixing with rain. "You are, you just don't see it. You think that Jane doesn't love Cameron because she doesn't act the way you think she should. Jane doesn't display her affections publicly, so whatever you failed to see wasn't there for a reason—Jane is shy. You of all people should recognize that!"

"I was protecting him!" He sucks in a ragged breath and lets it out slowly. A drizzling rain begins to fall, rapidly causing silvery drops to bead in his hair.

"Right, like you protected Grant's—"

He snorts.

My nostrils flare at his reaction. "Grant told me what you did to him. He told me everything about you."

"Really? I doubt that."

"He did."

"Wickham told you what favors him."

"I know you told him to stay away from me." I glare at him, hating him in that moment.

"You're not interested in hearing the truth."

"I already know it." I snatch his hand off my arm and take off for the stairs.

The drizzle turns to rain. Droplets roll down my face as I jog down the steps. At the last step, I break into a run. When I reach the fountain, I hear him yelling at my back.

"How can you judge my trying to protect my family, my reluctance to trust, when you know what I've been through?"

CHAPTER 30

In the arcade underneath the terrace and safe from the rain, I lean against one of the arches, gazing up at the intricate patterns on the ceiling tiles. I want to hear Darcy's story. I know I'm missing small pieces of a big puzzle. I can understand him not trusting, but I can't condone his actions. I can't empathize with the fact that he hides his heart so deeply he probably destroyed it.

I'm still there, standing at the bottom of the stairwell, pushing tears off my face when Darcy finds me. The arcade's lights cast a golden glow on Darcy's wet hair.

"I'm sorry. I won't trouble you again. I wish you well, Elizabeth." He turns to leave and steps out into the rain.

My heart is in my throat. I step forward, touching his arm lightly. He stops and turns to me. "Most people mistake my protection of Gwen for the desire to control her, but that's not it. I want you to understand." He takes a breath. "I need you to understand."

I look into his eyes and say, "I'm ready to listen."

His eyes soften, and innocence surfaces within their depths. I catch a glimpse of the little boy inside him. "My father was a corporate raider. You've heard about them. They lead a hostile takeover of a company, dissolve it, and then sell off the assets to generate profits."

I nod and fold my arms over my chest.

"My father was good at it, too good. He pissed off the wrong people, and they came after him." He pauses, swallowing thickly. "It was late at night, and I was sleeping. I was eight and Gwen was just a baby. I woke up to a loud crash downstairs and my mother flying into my bedroom with Gwen. She pushed me to the back of the closet and placed Gwen in my arms. She made me promise to stay in there no matter what I heard. I didn't understand why she was so scared until I heard gunshots. Gwen woke up and started crying. She told me to rock Gwen and keep her quiet. I begged her to hide with us. She kissed my cheek and then kissed Gwen's head. She told me to watch over Gwen and then she closed the door."

His face twists as he recalls the horror of what happened next. "The door didn't close completely, and I was too afraid to move. I saw everything. Two men crashed into the room and attacked my mother. Gwen started to cry again and I... I placed my hand over her little face."

He lets out a sob. Rain droplets slide from his hair to his cheeks mixing with tears. "I didn't want to hurt Gwen, but I didn't want the men to find us. I tried to keep her quiet. Her little face grew bright red. I thought I was hurting her, but I kept my hand over her mouth, keeping her quiet just like Mom told me to. I kept peeking through the crack hoping the men would leave. My mother was arguing with them saying she didn't know anything. One of them shoved her to her knees. And the other... The other man shot her in the back of the head."

My hand flies to my mouth.

He shakes his head, taking a shaky breath. "That's why I've always been protective of Gwen. I watched my parents die, unable to do anything about it. I've never felt so powerless, and I vowed never to feel like that ever again. I vowed to take care of Gwen, to watch over her. So when she got Meniere's disease, I convinced her to quit modeling."

"Meniere's disease?"

"It's an inner ear disorder that causes severe vertigo. It's also why I founded my biopharmaceutical company. I'm searching for a cure for her."

"Grant told me you made her quit because you didn't approve of her modeling."

"All I want is to see Gwen happy. I'd never intentionally take away something she loves to do. But the stress was making her disorder worse. She hated me for suggesting she quit, but she understood my reasoning. Grant didn't make it any easier for her either. He was her agent, profiting from her talent. He didn't care about her. He only cared about the money."

"So the story about you turning Gwen into an alcoholic because you made her quit?"

"A lie. When she gets vertigo, her world is off-balance. When she walks, it looks like she's drunk. Gwen's very private about her disorder, so she doesn't correct public misperceptions. An episode can come on suddenly, preventing her from driving, and I have to watch her carefully. I don't want her to get hurt."

I take a moment to take in everything he's saying. I remember the way he watched Gwen while she danced at the gala and Six Degrees.

"I want Gwen to do things that make her happy. Modeling no longer made her happy, but I realized that before she did. As much as I wish she would write in a different genre of novel, she seems fulfilled creating her mommy porn books."

"It's erotic romance not just for mommies." A smile slowly spreads across my face.

He gives me a whisper of a smile. "Right, erotic romance."

I bite my lip for a moment, thinking. "So, Grant lied to me."

"I'm afraid so."

"What about the rest? His parents? Did you really rob them?"

"Yes, that was me."

"You used your adoptive parents' money in a Ponzi scheme?"

"Not exactly." His gaze drops to his hands, making it apparent this is a painful story to tell. "When Grant realized he wouldn't make any more money off of Gwen, he looked for other ways he could turn a profit quickly. He accessed his parents' accounts draining them silently, nearly wiping them out."

I feel the corner of my mouth twitch as I swallow the urge to interrupt. At this point, I don't know if this story is fact or fiction. It's hard to know what's true and what's been added to play me.

Darcy swallows hard, avoiding my gaze as he finishes. "I tried to cover Grant's tracks by creating a paper trail to make it look like he took their money to invest it in a Ponzi scheme. When our father discovered the money was missing, I told him Grant was trying to increase their savings, but went about it the wrong way."

"Why would you do that?" I blink at him, gaping. He covered for Grant? The guy he so obviously hates? The story is passing the smell test because I don't see any reason why Darcy would cover for the guy. Maybe he has a soft spot I didn't see before.

Maybe he didn't want you to see it. The thought echoes in the back of my mind as his eyes meet mine.

His palms are facing up, his fingers are loosely tangled, as if he's trying not to wring his hands. "Because it would have broken our parents' hearts if they knew. Grant took their life savings and threw it away."

"So, Grant didn't keep the money?" Darcy shakes his head. "But why? That doesn't make any sense."

Unease grips Darcy's shoulders firmly and, in one shake, they drop. He looks to either side, lips parted, as if deciding whether or not to tell me more. "There are things I wanted to protect him from."

I scowl. "That's understandable, but it's also a lame answer. You can't tell me half a story and expect me to think there wasn't something nefarious going on—some reason you'd need to cover your own ass." Disappointed, I lower my face to the ground and am about to turn when he reaches for my arm, stopping me.

The touch is light, then his hands return to his sides. His eyes rake my face, trying to decide something. He blinks and words follow. "It's not my secret, nor my shame. I don't want to make things harder for Grant. I'm trusting you with information about my family that has the potential to cause more pain than you could possibly imagine." He swallows hard, takes a deep breath and meets my eyes. "It has nothing to do with me. I know it's not possible to save people, but it's not like me to give up on them either. Grant stole our parent's money to get high. He's addicted to cocaine—has been for a while."

I tear my gaze away and repress the urge to pace and tick off things on my fingers. Was I seriously alone with a crackhead without realizing it? He was a little moody, okay very moody, but he was also insanely hot so I let it slide. I thought he had guy PMS not a drug problem.

Darcy keeps spilling his secrets, not stopping, not waiting for me to pass judgment. "That's also why I told him to stay away from you. I threatened to tell our parents the truth about the real reason the money went missing. Thank God it worked, but it hurts that he believes I'd go through with it. The Wickhams raised Gwen and me as if we were their own. I could never hurt them like that."

I stare at him, wondering if I know this man at all. I open my mouth, but have no idea what to say.

"Beth, when you overheard me speaking with Cameron at the Degatto's charity gala, I was fighting against my attraction to you."

"Why?"

The corner of his mouth pulls up into a crooked smile and he shakes his head. "I wouldn't usually have said anything like that, but your mother had just announced to the room that she was hunting for billionaire husbands for her daughters. Between that and Cameron's history of helping me, I was trying to bow out gracefully. I had no idea you were there. I'm so sorry."

My heart is twisting inside of my chest. He thought I was attractive? Really?

I ignore that train of thought. I have no freaking clue what station I'll end up at.

I redirect toward the woman always at the center of everything, like it or not. "I'm sorry, I know that my mother can be... There are no words for her. I can see why you had your guard up that night and probably since then. There is nothing comparable to my mother's mouth."

William moves closer to me and my breath catches with surprise. His eyes lock with mine as he speaks. "Then I saw you with Colin Frey, and I was jealous. I wanted to be the one to make you laugh and act silly. I wanted to be the one you lean on, the one you look to when you need help. I desperately wanted to be the one you cling to when you feel alone."

His incredible blue eyes drift toward my lips as his hand comes to my face. I wonder if he's going to stroke my cheek, but he doesn't. Instead he tucks a wet strand of hair behind my ear. He leans in slowly, lips parting. I hold my breath as the space between us closes. His warm breath cascades over my skin making my lips part in response.

The kiss is charged and I can already feel the current surging through me. The memory of his mouth on mine, of those sinful lips on my body sends an undeniable jolt through me—this is more than lust. I want tender kisses, not just hot devouring caresses from this man. A tremble begins somewhere inside of me, ripping through my body at the thought. I want to run, but my feet won't move. That kiss is too important. It'll change everything.

He lingers waiting for me, allowing me to be the one to decide where this relationship goes. My pulse races, deafening the sounds of the sky tearing in two, drowning out the rain and thunder. It's only me and Darcy.

The vibration of my phone shakes me back to reality.

Darcy's eyes are glassy. His gaze drifts to the phone.

MOM: WHERE ARE YOU!

What is she talking about? Oh, God! The engagement. I forgot.

"Colin."

Darcy freezes as I whisper my friend's name. Hurt floods his handsome face, and he pulls back. "You love him."

"Yes, I do, but it's not—"

"Forgive me for burdening you with all of this. I won't mention it again."

I watch him walk away, his proud shoulders slumped. I want to go to him, to tell him to come back. I can't.

Without a word, he turns and disappears into the dark rainy night.

I fall back against the wall, my knees too weak to hold my weight anymore. I want to laugh. I want to cry. I think I'm going crazy. I want to run after him and tell him I'm an idiot. I want to tell him off for making me come dangerously close to falling for him.

The truth is I fell for him a long time ago. Maybe I did see the real William Darcy all those times? My own stupidity blinded me to it.

My phone buzzes again, and I snatch it out of my pocket with half a mind to throw it in a puddle. I glimpse at the screen and in an instant, I'm running full-speed out of the arcade.

MARY: Dad's at Mount Sinai Hospital. Come quick!

CHAPTER 31

There's a woman I don't know sitting on Dad's hospital bed. She looks like my mother, but instead of perfectly coiffed hair, this woman's hair is lifeless and flat, her skin devoid of makeup. My mother never leaves the apartment without her "face" on.

Jane and Mary sit in the corner of the room. Jane's sobbing and Mary has an arm around her, trying to comfort her.

"David, I'm so sorry," the woman's voice croaks. "I tried. I really did."

"Mother?" I can't believe it's her. The mother I know doesn't cry in public. She doesn't express anything resembling love.

Weepy hazel eyes turn to lock on mine, and I glimpse the mother I remember from childhood. The mother who rocked me to sleep when I was sick, kissed my boo-boos, and braided my hair while she told me I could be whatever I wanted when I grew up. Somehow, somewhere, that mother disappeared, and I forgot she ever existed.

Her face shifts and her more familiar stern features reappear. She wipes the tears from her cheeks, stiffening her shoulders before she speaks. "Beth, we've been trying to reach you all evening."

"I'm sorry. What happened?"

"Beth?" A weak voice croaks so softly that it's barely audible.

I rush to the bed at the sound of Dad's voice. He sounds so fragile. "Dad?"

"Remember what I told you about your mother," he says. I glance back at her. The stern expression is gone and tears glisten in her eyes as she gazes at him lovingly.

"Please, David. Don't talk. I'll take care of everything." Mother cups his pale cheek. "You rest."

Dad's brown eyes look at Mother tenderly as he continues. "Beth, she's the love of my life. Never forget that." His voice falters as his head drops, and he loses consciousness.

"Dad!" I freak out, shaking his shoulder. "Dad!"

"Let him sleep, Beth," Mother says.

"What's wrong with him?" I look to Mary.

Mary shakes her head. Her eyes are puffy and rimmed with redness. She's been crying and swatting away tears, trying to convince herself this nightmare isn't happening. Because it's not nothing. Anyone that looks at Dad can see this isn't something minor.

Mary clears her throat. "Mother wanted to wait until we were all here to tell us."

"Well, we're here, tell us." From the expression on Mother's face, I know this is the secret. This is what they've been keeping from us since I returned to New York.

"There's no easy way to say this. Your father has been sick for some time. His kidneys are failing, both of them. He's been on the transplant list for a while now, but if he doesn't get one soon, he'll . . . he'll . . ." she bursts into tears.

My heart plummets to my stomach, and I can't breathe. The room grows still as I take in the meaning of what Mother's telling us. It's like everything is in slow motion. Jane's face transforms into someone I don't recognize. Her mouth drops open as if screaming, but nothing comes out.

Mary is a statue. From beneath thick black bangs, soft brown eyes widen in terror. It's the same expression she had when she lost Sofia. Then her eyes narrow and her red lips press into a thin line.

"I have a kidney." Mary's voice sounds strained, as if she's fighting against breaking down. "Where do I sign up? Come on, Mother. We're wasting time crying. Let's find a surgeon. Now!"

Mother jumps at Mary's harsh tone and, just this once, I feel bad for her. "Mary, I think it's more complicated than that. If it were that easy, Dad would've gotten a transplant already. Right? It's not that simple, is it?"

Mother looks at me gratefully as she dabs a tissue around her eyes. "No, it isn't. We've been searching for a match, but none of us are a fit. He's been on dialysis, and it worked for a while, but then he started getting worse." She starts to cry again as the words rush out of her. "Insurance didn't cover half of the expenses and... and we used up all our savings. We borrowed against the mortgage on the apartment and on the company's holdings, and now it looks like we will lose everything—including your father."

"Whoa, Mother, slow down. How long has Dad been on dialysis?"

"Twenty-five months."

"Two years!" Mary screams. "You had Dad on dialysis for two fucking years?"

Mary spits out a slew of curses. Jane's lips are moving, but I can't hear what she's saying.

"Mary, calm down. Jane's trying to talk."

Mary huffs, folding her arms across her chest.

"Mother, why didn't you tell us about this before? Why didn't you tell us when Dad went to the hospital a few months ago, when Beth moved back home?" Jane speaks carefully, calmly even though she's splintering apart inside.

"Your father didn't want any of you to know. Neither of us wanted to put you through this."

"You don't have to do this alone," Jane's eyes are big as she holds Mother's gaze. "We're family."

Mother lets out a sob. Jane pats her back as Mother cries into her chest. "I wanted my girls to have good lives. I didn't want you to worry about us. I tried. I was so sure I could find someone to care for each of you financially. We have nothing left to give you."

My jaw drops. "Is that why you've spent the last few months dragging us to galas hunting for billionaires? To find someone to care for us? Mother, we can take care of ourselves. Spending all that money on sundresses and gowns," I temper my words and simply ask, "What were you thinking?"

Mother blows her nose, shaking her head. "I only bought clothes for Jane when she went to Cameron's to paint the mural."

"But I saw you with shopping bags all the time."

Mother's face flushes a bright pink. "They were empty. Sometimes I put my own clothes in the bags, and when I went shopping with Catherine Degatto, I returned each purchase the next day."

"Why would you do that?"

"I had to keep up appearances. No man of wealth would go near any of you if they thought we were poor. They'd think we were only after their money."

I shake my head, unable to process the flawed logic without being cruel. Mary's been leaning in the doorway, arms over her chest and fails to maintain her anger. She's the first with a chuckle, closely followed by Jane's high-pitched giggle. Then we're all laughing.

Tears stream down my face, I'm laughing so hard. I'm laughing at the crazy that is my life. Dad keeps a secret from us, risking his life not to worry us. Mother pretends to be rich so we can marry into wealth. And me, agreeing to marry my gay best friend so he can pretend to be straight. When did life get so messed up?

"It's not funny," Mother says over our laughter.

"I know it's not," I finally say when I catch my breath. I pad over to her and place my hand on her shoulder. "I love you, I don't say it enough, but I do. And if I'm ever in a bad spot, I know I want you fighting for me."

She offers a weak smile and pats her nose with a tissue. "I am fighting for you, for all of you. I thought if we had some of the finances smoothed out, it wouldn't be so difficult."

"You're not alone anymore, Ma." I tease her, calling her the pet name from happier times.

She holds my hand and squeezes it hard. "I know and I'm so thankful you stayed."

CHAPTER 32

We all have tests run to double check, but there's still no match. Dad's body doesn't have even the slightest chance of accepting my kidney, Mary's or Jane's. Mary's frustrated scream after being told she couldn't help is haunting. I hear it long after the echo fades.

Dr. Wade is explaining things to us. Jane and Mother ask a few questions while Mary glares at the doctor, arms folded over her chest.

"Have faith, Ms. Bennet." Dr. Wade shoots Mary a confident smile. "There's time and opportunity for a miracle yet."

He leaves, and I sink back into my chair. It feels like all the air left the room with Dr. Wade. I want to scream, to march down to the nurse's station and throw things until they find a way to fix this. All I can do is stare.

Movement in the corner of my eye catches my attention, and I watch as Mother rushes to the door. "I need some fresh air and a cup of coffee," she says, turning the knob. "Do you need anything?"

The words seem to reverberate within the room. I need to save our home. I need to save our company. I need to save Dad. How am I not a match? I'm the most like him—same eyes, same hair, same coloring. Why won't my kidney save his life?

"No, Mother. Thank you."

She smiles at me from the doorway, unshed tears glistening in her eyes. "You've done all you can, Beth. Now we wait. We haven't lost him yet." Her voice cracks and a sob escapes her lips. She runs from the room, the door slamming shut behind her.

Mother and I haven't left Dad's side for days. While Mary and Jane take turns camping at Dad's office, doing what they can to keep his business running, Mother and I stationed ourselves in the chairs on either side of his bed. He floats in and out of consciousness and, in those few precious moments he's awake, we tell him we love him.

Mary, Jane, and I pooled all our savings, money from any account we could think of. It isn't much. It feels like even less after our conversation with hospital billing. We owe hundreds of thousands of dollars, a total that's rapidly increasing each day.

I pull out my phone to text Colin. I only say I need to talk with him. It pains me to ask him for money, but for Dad, for the sake of my family, I have to.

———

Later in the evening, I'm still in my chair in Dad's hospital room, re-reading one of Gwen's novels on my phone. At Dad's insistence, Mother went back to the apartment for a quick nap. I promised I'd call her if anything changed.

"Beth! We've got great news," Jane says as she and Mary rush into the room. "We just got back from hospital billing. They called us in to let us know the hospital has given us a grant large enough to cover all our hospital bills—including Dad's transplant! Well, after it comes."

"Are you serious?" Relief hits me like a two by four, and I let out a rush of air. The knots in my stomach untie and I sink back into the chair. "That's great, but I don't remember applying for a grant? I didn't even know the hospital awarded grant money."

"That's what I said," Mary says as she walks briskly toward me, a smile on her face and a bounce in her step. I haven't seen her happy in too long. No, it's not happy—it's hopeful.

"What did they tell you about the grant?"

Mary shrugs as she sits on the windowsill, looking down at the cars in the parking lot below. "They said the hospital gets donations from time to time. Bestowing a grant to a family in need is not unusual and can be done at their discretion."

Something doesn't sound right. I have the worst luck in the world, followed by the rest of my family, so how'd we win the jackpot here? I feel my brow wrinkle and try not to sound ungrateful, but I have to know. "Why'd they choose us?"

"Does it matter?" Jane's voice is sharp. She followed Mary inside and has been standing at the foot of Dad's bed, arms folded around her middle as if cold, eyes narrow and careful. I've never seen her so defensive, so afraid. "As long as it's helping Dad, who cares where it comes from."

Mary tries to hide her shock and turns back to the pane of glass, but I see her reflection—how her young face crumples in pain seeing her sister's gentleness washed away in a matter of days. It was Jane's trademark quality. Even while everyone else loses their shit, Jane is always sweet and gentle. To hear the bark in her voice stings.

"I'm sorry," Jane says quickly, seeing our reaction. "I didn't mean to..." Her voice trails off and her breath hitches.

"It's okay, Jane. You can't repress awesomeness like that for decades and expect it not to slip out every now and again. Besides, I like this bold, new Jane."

"Me too," Mary chimes in, following my lead. "The next time you see Cameron, you can rip him a new one."

Jane's eyes well with tears at the mention of Cameron's name. She still hasn't heard from him. With all that's happened with Dad, I'm no longer certain who she's crying for—probably both of them.

Blinking back tears, she forces a smile to her face. "There's more good news. The hospital placed Dad on the top of the transplant list this afternoon and they've already found a donor." She beams at us, barely able to keep her smile contained to her face. It's like Jane ate a spoonful of sunshine.

"They did?" I push up from my slouch, hanging on her every word.

Jane nods. "They're going to do the transplant operation tomorrow morning. Dr. Wade will be by soon with more details. I'm not supposed to know. I sort of overheard it while I wasn't eavesdropping on the nurses in the hallway." She shoots us a sheepish smile.

Mary laughs and drops a booted foot to the floor while draping her arm over the other knee, still half perched on the windowsill. "Jane, I'm supposed to be the badass punk in the family! Get your own MO."

"Do you think it's true? I mean, it wasn't speculation? Dad's locked it?" I ask Jane.

She nods. "It's legit. I saw her typing it into the computer as the surgeon told her about it. The kidney is from an organ donor who died today in a wreck. It's being flown here now."

I start shaking and cover my mouth with my hands. Tears form in my eyes and I laugh. "It's over?"

Jane walks over to me, arms spread wide, and nods. "It's over. Everything is going to be all right." She embraces me for a moment before I feel Mary plow into us. The three of us stay there for a moment, hugging, crying, and laughing the pain away.

———

I want to share the good news, so I pull out my phone to call Mother but see an unsent text from earlier. I thought I asked Colin to call me, but it's still there, unsent. I frown, my brain falling down a rabbit hole of questions as I settle back into the chair.

This morning, none of us were a match, and our only option was to wait for a miracle. By this evening, not only has Dad moved to the top of the transplant list, but they've also found a donor, and we've been awarded a grant to pay for it. Something feels fishy about this. My first suspicion would have been Colin—that he'd used Frey Oil money to save us—but he still doesn't know for sure that none of us are a match. I told him we were being tested to make sure there wasn't an error previously.

I look up at my sisters. "Not to sound like an ass, but... I'm relieved about the grant and the donor, and, of course, we'll accept help from wherever it's offered to save Dad, but..." I pause trying to figure out the best way to say it. "Haven't you guys wondered how this happened so quickly?"

At my question, Mary looks at Jane and ducks her head. Jane's eyes dart to the side and she turns away, rubbing the back of her neck.

I slam my feet to the floor and practically jump out of the chair. "You know! OMG! How could you not tell me?"

Jane rolls her shoulder and offers a smug look, while Mary smirks at me from behind those dark bangs.

I'm on my feet, charging toward them. "Spill it! What else do you two know?"

Mary jumps up next to Jane to try and ask something, but I don't let her. "Tell me. Now." From the way she's acting, it's got to be something awful. Like the grant money came from human trafficking or something.

Mary swallows hard and tries to look at Jane. I step between them. "Mary?"

She breaks. "Fine, we overheard some nurses talking about a massive donation. They said that the hospital received it earlier today from an unexpected source."

"Who?"

Jane places her small hand on my shoulder, so I turn to look at her. Her eyes are kind again, careful as if this might hurt me.

"The money came from the Darcy Foundation."

I freeze in place as the world falls to my feet, crashing against the linoleum like a giant gong. My jaw hangs open and words fail me.

Mary raises an eyebrow at my reaction. "Well, that caught your attention real quick."

She studies me as I try to play it off. "What else did they say?"

"They were talking about a condition of the donation—that a portion of the money be used anonymously to pay the debts of a particular patient in full. If this patient weren't made an immediate priority, there would be no money at all. Apparently, the donation is build-a-new-wing huge, and the hospital administrators were more than willing to agree to get their hands on the larger gift."

"The patient?"

Jane presses her lips lightly and replies. "Considering the timing, that patient has to be Dad." She pauses, thinking. "If it wasn't Darcy, who else do we know who could afford to do this for us? I don't know any billionaires willing to stick their neck out for us other than Colin. Maybe Cameron, but he's on my shitlist until he grows the balls to explain why he ran out on me."

"About Cameron," I begin, "it's not entirely his fault—"

"Beth, Jane, look! Dad's waking up." Mary calls out.

I move to let them have time with Dad and tell him the good news. I don't know how I'm going to explain all of this to Mary or Jane. They don't know how I feel about him, though I'm certain they suspect the truth. They also don't know Cameron planned on proposing, but Darcy talked him out of it—and into breaking up with her instead. Maybe they'll think Darcy donated the money to the hospital out of guilt. I don't think so. Something tells me it's more than that, especially since he did it anonymously. It was by chance we found out about it at all.

I force myself to push all thoughts of Darcy aside. I'll have time to think about all this later. Right now, it's time to focus on my family.

CHAPTER 33

"You know, Beth, I like that shade of green on you." Colin points to the mud mask on my face. "It brings out the color of your eyes."

"Knock it off, Colin." I dip my spoon into my cereal. "Some of us don't have naturally perfect skin like you or Jane."

Jane smiles. "You're so sweet, Beth."

"Sweet nothing. It's the truth." I watch Jane poke at her plate of fruit.

Dad's surgery was a success, and he's getting stronger each day, but as life gets back to normal, Jane is finding it difficult to get over Cameron. Helping at Dad's office only provides her a little bit of a distraction. As much as it pains me, I encourage her to help Mother and Mrs. Frey with wedding plans. Anything to keep her busy.

Oddly enough, neither Jane nor Mary says much about me actually following through to marry a man

I don't love. They seem sad about it, but they don't question me, tell me I'm crazy, or anything else. It's like they understand why I'm doing it.

I can't let him go up in flames. I can't let his family destroy him. I'm the only one who can stand between them, and I'm hoping that's enough.

It's early in the morning and we're all sitting around the breakfast table—even Colin, who has always been more comfortable with my family than I am.

Only Colin and my mother are fully dressed, the rest of us enjoying breakfast in the clothes we slept in. Mary's wearing boxers and a faded black Ramones concert t-shirt. Jane has pink curlers dangling from the ends of her hair and a matching frilly, nightshirt that pokes out from beneath a cotton candy colored robe. I'm wearing a tank top, pajama pants, and a bright green mud mask. It's female central.

"Colin, you must help me convince your mother to pick the table centerpieces first." Mother dabs the corners of her mouth with a napkin as she finishes her brioche. "We can't even think of the décor for the rest of the ballroom until we have the centerpieces selected." We were all shocked when Mother agreed to help Mrs. Frey plan the wedding, even graciously accepting Mrs. Frey's offer to foot the entire bill without protest.

OVER YOU

Mary slurps loudly, gulping the remaining milk from her bowl. "Mother's right," she says sarcastically, milk dripping from her chin onto the table. "It's all about the centerpieces. No one gives a fuck about the bride anymore. That's so 2015." She waves a jaunty wrist and giggles.

Colin stifles a laugh as Jane snorts fruit out her nostrils.

"Mary! Mind your manners!" Mother frowns, scolding her youngest daughter. But it's softened when she kisses Mary's forehead before grabbing a dishrag off the counter.

Colin nibbles at a piece of rice bread with cinnamon sugar on it. "Don't worry, Mrs. Bennet. I agree completely. You know, maybe I should call you Mother Bennet?"

I try not to laugh, because it rolls right off the tongue and plummets like a stone to the floor. "What a lovely idea." I put my elbows on the table and fold my fingers together, watching the conversation unfold.

"I'd love that," Mother beams. "I'm excited about the wedding. I'm so glad it's coming so soon, and we don't have to wait two years like most of New York insists on doing. Thank God your mother's a Texan. An engagement lasting more than a month down there is half way to forever. Planning an event like this so quickly is a challenge, but I know we can do it. It's been a rough few weeks for us, and we can certainly use some—dear, Lord!"

There's a loud flapping and a tiny gray object zooms through the kitchen. Mother ducks, screaming and waving the dishrag at the object.

"Lucy! I told you to wait in our room!" Mary cries, scowling at the bird. "You're so impatient."

The pigeon lands on the table. She tilts her head to the side watching Mother duck behind the counter in a panic. "A bird, Mary? You let a bird into the apartment?"

"Mother, you're overreacting," Jane says as she gently strokes the pigeon's head. "Sweet little Lucy wouldn't hurt anyone. Would you, Lucy?"

Mother's eyes grow wide. "You named her after my mother!"

Mary places her tattooed arms behind her head, locking her hands. "Yep. She looks like Grams, don't you think? Tiny, plump, gray hair."

"I wouldn't figure you to be the type to cage a bird in your room," Colin says to Mary. He takes a big bite of his rice bread and mumbles, "Aren't you more of a free-range, cage-free, it's-better-in-the-wild kind of activist?"

"I don't keep her caged." Mary swipes a few of the crumbs falling from Colin's plate and throws it to Lucy. "I tried letting her go. She keeps coming back. That's not my fault."

"Mmm, these are delicious, Mother Bennet. Did you make this loaf?"

"Thank you, Colin. Yes, I did," Mother replies, popping up from behind the counter.

I shake my head at Mother's reply and whisper, "Bakery down the street."

"Stop feeding the bird!" Mother cries at Jane. "That's why she keeps coming back."

"But she's hungry." Mary gives Mother a look that says of course we have to feed her. Who else will?

The doorbell rings, and I push myself from the table, chuckling as Mary and Mother continue arguing. I can't believe I actually missed this.

"I'll get it. It's probably Sandra. She said she'd bring by the documents Dad wanted to see before she goes into the office this morning."

When I open the door, my mouth falls open in shock. Cameron and Darcy are standing in the foyer.

I stop. My legs won't move. William Darcy looks unbelievably sexy in a simple sports coat and jeans. Were his eyes always so incredibly blue? Coupled with the dark hair falling in his eyes, he's breathtakingly beautiful. He's smiling kindly, unguarded as if he thinks no one is watching. That's when he glances up and his eyes lock with mine, my heart tries to skip over beats and trips, landing somewhere in my socks.

Darcy blinks with surprise, and then his lips twitch slightly.

My hands fly up to my mud mask. I let out a yelp, slamming the door closed in their faces.

"Who was that?" Mother asks, visibly trying not to scold me for slamming the door.

"It's Cameron and Darcy." I say his last name as if it'll conjure a spell to keep him out of my heart. As if last names keep people distant and unloved.

Do I love him? Where'd that come from? Panic settles in my stomach. Colin's here. Darcy is here. And, dear God, what does Cameron want?

"No." Mother's voice comes out in a shocked whisper. Jane turns greener than my mask.

"Yes. I'm afraid so, Jane." I'm going to puke. I keep my back to the door and press my palms against the cool wood.

Mother gasps as her eyes bounce from me to Jane. "Everyone stay calm."

Calm? How can I stay calm? I just slammed the door in Darcy's face. Eventually, someone is going to open it, and I'll have to face him again. What will I say? Oops, my hand slipped?

I'm as anxious as Jane looks.

With her composure regained, Mother starts barking orders. "Jane, go change. Beth, you'll help her. Mary, take that...that..."

"Lucy," Mary says patiently.

"Dear, Lord! Take Lucy to your room. I'll bring Mr. Bingley and Mr. Darcy into the sitting room."

As I trail behind Jane to our room, I hear Mother say, "Colin would you mind helping me entertain?"

When mother's back is to me, I frantically shake my head at Colin. He can't be alone with Darcy. "That's a bad plan," I mouth to my best friend.

He ignores me. "Not at all, Mother Bennet. I love entertaining men!" He sounds so flamboyantly gay that I wonder how she doesn't know.

"Colin!" I shoot a death stare at him, but he just smiles in return and goes into the sitting room.

"Mother, don't you think—"

"Go help Jane and join us after you're dressed." She's got rosy cheeks and a smile on her face that practically sings 'double wedding.'

After Mary forces Lucy back into her room, she joins Jane and me, watching us run frantically around the room as we dress. "I know why Jane's freaking out, but what's your excuse, Beth?"

I wipe a wet towel over my face, rubbing off the remainder of the mud mask. I try to keep my voice steady, but the words come out way too fast. "I'm not freaking out. What makes you think I'm freaking out? They caught me off guard, that's all, and I'm excited for Jane. Cameron's finally back. Can you believe it? Aren't you excited? I'm excited." I'm talking too fast.

Mary raises an eyebrow. "Uh, huh. And your sounding like Alvin from The Chipmunks on a caffeine high and putting on that sexy red blouse has nothing to do with William Darcy sitting in our living room. Sure."

My face heats up and turns almost the same shade as my blouse. I go into the closet, reminding myself to breathe, and dig out a pair of dress slacks and matching heels. "No, not at all."

"Are you still concerned about what Grant told you about him?" Jane's delicate features pinch with worry. "Maybe we should send them both away."

"No!" Mary and I yell in unison.

"It's not that," I say, letting out a breath. I sink onto the bed next to her. "Jane, I was wrong about him. You were right. Darcy's a very kind and thoughtful man."

Jane's perfectly arched brows rise in surprise. "So what Grant told you wasn't true?"

"No. That rat-bastard lied to me. A lot." I frown, thinking about it. Sometimes it's easier to believe pretty lies than ugly truth.

"I was wrong about him, too," Mary jumps in and then adds, "I'm certain he's the reason for everything at the hospital. If Darcy were the evil corporate puppet I thought he was, he wouldn't have taken the time to help people like us. We're ants compared to him, but for some reason he saw we needed help and stepped up."

"That's true," Jane says nodding.

"It's especially true, since the only one of us he really likes is Beth." She waggles her eyebrows at me, grinning.

"Hey!" I feel my face flush again.

Jane's pink lips curve into a delicate smile. "We'll have to figure out a way to thank him."

"That man is despicable. Will Darcy, corporate overlord and company undertaker by day, all around badass hero by night. He obviously needs his own Bat Signal." With a giggle from Jane and Mary, we stand and walk out of the bedroom.

Jane and Mary rush past me, leaving me alone with my thoughts to walk down the hall. This is insane. I don't know what's come over me. I'm acting like Darcy's here to see me. He's probably here to inquire after Dad, and Cameron obviously came to see Jane. I knew Cameron would come, eventually.

As I get closer, I can hear Mother talking animatedly about the wedding. My heart sinks as I wonder what Darcy thinks of me. He doesn't know Colin's sexual orientation, and this conversation probably pains him—assuming his feelings in the arcade were genuine.

I don't see how they could be anything else. I remember the look on his face, the pain in his eyes.

"There she is," Mother says as I stroll into the sitting area last and close the doors behind me. She sighs contently. "Now we can begin."

I find a seat next to Mary and feel Darcy's eyes on the side of my face. He's sitting awkwardly in a small chaise next to Cameron.

The room stills. Slowly, Cameron rises to his feet. His eyes grow wide, drinking in Jane and her peach-colored, ruffled, silk blouse and matching pants. Her silky hair falls in soft waves around her shoulders.

"Jane," he breathes, staring at her as if she might disappear.

"Cameron," Jane's voice is a whisper. Gone is the bossy tyrant from the hospital. Although she still has more backbone, she's lost the accompanying sharp tongue. "You shouldn't be here. We have nothing more to say."

They stand gazing at each other, for a moment, but as soon as Jane's words hit his ears, Cameron pales. He parts his lips as if he's going to speak once, then again, but he says nothing.

Awkwardness descends like a thick blanket, so mother torches it. There won't be a moment of uncomfortable silence, not in her home. "That outfit looks lovely on you, Jane," Mother offers, and then turns to her guests. "Don't you think so, Mr. Bingley?"

Cameron smiles at Jane, flashing a dimple. "It does Mrs. Bennet. Jane is breathtaking today."

"Thank you," Jane says, a delicate pink flushing her pretty cheeks.

Darcy stands, clearing his throat, and addressing the room, "Your mother says your father is doing well after his surgery." It's unclear if he's talking to me or one of my sisters.

Mary replies, "Yes, he is doing much better. We should be able to bring him home soon."

Darcy smiles softly, before lifting his eyes to meet mine. I see a struggle behind them. It's as if he wants to tell me something. His gaze flicks to Colin then back to me, his face schooled into a polite mask.

"He'll be out in time for Colin and Beth's wedding. Though I doubt he'll be able to manage walking her down the aisle," Mother explains. "You and Cameron must come, and bring your lovely sister, too. It'll be the social event of the year."

Disappointment flashes across Darcy's face so fast, I think I've imagined it.

From the corner of my eye, I catch a bewildered look from Colin. He never misses a thing, but I've kept this so deeply buried there's no way he could know. Plus he's never seen us together to get clued in.

Until today.

Until this moment.

"Thank you, Mrs. Bennet. I'm sure Gwen will be delighted. If you'll excuse me, I have some business I need to attend to, and I know Cameron wants to speak with Jane." Darcy gives Cameron a nudge.

"Uh, yes. That's right," Cameron says. "I was wondering if I could speak with Jane alone."

"Jane," Mary begins, "why don't you take Cameron to Dad's den while I show Mr. Darcy out?"

I stay glued to my spot, willing my feet to move. I want to tell Darcy to stay. I want to tell him I was totally wrong about him—about everything. But there's no point. It'll only cause us both pain, so I stay in my spot, my lips sealed.

When he passes by me, I glance up at him. Blue eyes gaze into mine, searching, waiting, hoping. When I say nothing more, he lets out a breath, nodding as he says my name, "Elizabeth."

I've never been cut in two like that before. It's elating and crushing at the same time. The caress of my full name and the way he says it with those perfectly pink lips brings back the other things he's said, the things we've done. But I know he'll keep his promise and never bother me again. He'll stay out of my life from now on, and that was his official goodbye.

I sit there trying to hide my heart as the room explodes in chatter. Everyone knows what Cameron is asking, and I'm happy for Jane. The two of them will be so happy together, but it feels like I'm lost in a bubble, floating away. One day I'll be out of reach, and this moment won't seem so difficult.

A few minutes later, a squeal comes from Dad's den. I'm getting up to check on them, when Cameron and Jane return, hand in hand, to the living room, huge smiles plastered across their faces.

"What in the world is going on?" Mother asks coyly, as if she's been sitting and reading a magazine the entire time with no suspicions.

Mary marches to Jane and lifts her left hand. "Bocce Balls! Cameron finally grew a pair and asked you to marry him."

"Yes!" Jane squeals.

Everyone starts talking at once. I rush over and give her a hug, then gawk at her ring. Her face lights up making her look even more beautiful. When my eyes meet Colin's I smile, but he sees through me. He still has that puzzled look on his face, watching me fiddle with my own engagement ring. Most of the time, I don't even realize I have it on. Today, I feel its weight, and it's heavy.

CHAPTER 34

"Hey, why aren't you at the Ritz-Carlton yet?" Mary walks into the sitting room with Lucy perched on her hand.

"I was already there, and left." I frown. "I had to take a break from Mother and Mrs. Frey. It's crazy in stereo over there. Even Jane's getting irritated," I say, taking off my shoes. "I told Mother I had to get dressed for this evening. Besides, I wanted to check in on Dad. How is he?"

"I finally got him off the computer. He's napping."

We brought Dad home from the hospital a few days ago. He's feeling so well, Mary and I have to watch him like a hawk to make sure he doesn't over do it. He's already tried to go to the office twice. When we shipped him back to bed, he resigned to working from the study.

Mary paces the room, petting Lucy while she walks. Her voice is flat, but urgent. "So, I know that I'm the little sis, but I wanted to make sure that you had all your cookies in the jar."

Perplexed I look at her. "What?"

"You know the window for getting out of this scam is quickly closing, right?" Mary strokes the feathers lightly, making the little bird coo.

"I don't know what you're talking about."

"Come on, Beth. You're hot for William Darcy."

"I am not."

"Uh, huh." She rubs Lucy's head with short black-lacquered fingernails.

"You're being ridiculous."

"I'm being ridiculous?" Mary laughs. "I'm not the one tossing aside one of the few nice guys in the city—a man who happens to have the hots for you, too, by the way—to marry my gay best friend."

I don't drop my jaw in shock fast enough. I don't protest or act insulted. I just melt and wish it were over.

"Ah, ha! I knew it."

I don't look at her. How can I? I feel like a hypocrite. "It doesn't matter."

"Of course it does! Beth, this isn't an episode of The Bold and The Brainless. Call it off with Colin and live a long, sexually fulfilled life with Will and his willy instead."

~271~

Even her over the top remarks don't make me laugh, not today. The wedding is only a few days away. Invitations have been sent and a great deal of money has been spent. It's too late to walk away.

I shake my head. "I promised Colin I'd marry him."

"Colin needs to grow up. So his parents might cut him off the family tree. Boo, hoo. Why does he want to stay with a family who doesn't love him for who he truly is? If they can't accept him, they don't deserve him. Colin always has us. We're his family. He loses nothing by coming clean—you lose everything!"

"You're wrong, Mary. Colin will lose everything. The life he knows will vanish and he'll be shamed so publicly it'll destroy him. It's why I said yes in the first place. I can do this."

"No you can't. Beth, don't throw away what you have with Darcy. Don't make me stage a picket-loving protest against Frey Oil on your wedding day, because I'll do it."

Colin and I agreed to have the media present at the nuptials. There are still some rumors flying around about Colin's sexual orientation. He decided having a little makeout session in front of the media would help squelch the rumors. I'm not looking forward to it. Interrupting it with media coverage of my activist sister crashing the party with a protest makes the whole situation seem worse.

"Thanks, but I gave my word. I won't break it."

"Marrying Colin is a mistake, Beth. I wish I could make you see."

"It was you who pushed me to say yes in the first place!"

"That was before I knew you were madly in love with William Darcy. Love changes everything."

"No," I smile sadly at her. "It doesn't. That's where the storybooks are wrong. That's where the dream falls flat because in the end, love doesn't matter. Loyalty supersedes everything, and if you know me at all, you'll realize that I won't betray my family—that includes Colin. So I'll walk down the aisle and I don't want to hear you mention William Darcy again. I can't deal with it, Mary. Promise me."

Her young face is frozen in disagreement, but she manages a nod. "I promise, Beth."

CHAPTER 35

I thought I was ready for this. I thought I could do it. It takes everything I have not to run screaming as Colin guides me into the main ballroom at the Ritz by the Park.

It's February 13th, and very cold outside. Somehow, Mr. Frey was able to book the main ballroom for tonight and tomorrow—Valentine's Day—with almost no notice. The perks of being richer than God never end. Jane heard Mrs. Frey paid the couple that originally booked the venue handsomely to hand over the date quietly. Apparently, the Freys paid for two weddings this month.

As I step into the ballroom, my jaw drops. The wedding coordinator ushers us in, taking my vintage fur shrug Mr. Frey gave me as an engagement present as we pass. Mary almost stroked out over the gift. I'm surprised she didn't paint the white fox fur red on the way to the limo. I told her we could bury it in the yard as soon as the wedding is over. That appeased her for now.

Vintage furs belonged to animals that would have died before Mary was born, but Mary still wouldn't be okay with wearing them if it were road kill fur. I'm glad she has firm beliefs and stands by them.

As I step into the ballroom, I gasp. Putting my hand to my heart, I breathe, "Oh, Colin, this is beautiful!"

Everything is decorated in pale shades of orange with shimmering silver accents and birch branches. Crystals hang from tall topiaries with willowy, pale branches, catching the light perfectly. It feels like I'm walking through a silver forest. Tables are dressed in whites and silvers with pale flowers draped and flowing over antique candelabras. It's beyond beautiful.

"This is nothing. Wait until you see what they've done for tomorrow." He knows that I gave free reign to our mothers to go nuts. I only asked that they keep things serene and short as possible. "It'll blow your mind."

"I'm sure it will." Seriously, this feels like a fairytale and it'd be lovely except I'm marrying a guy that might as well be my brother. I feel like I should hang a sign above my cooch: OUT OF BUSINESS.

I feel so sad and the ballroom looks so pretty that my mood turns melancholy. My sudden tears are mistaken for blushing bridal emotion.

I'm starting to think the rehearsal dinner is going to outshine the wedding when white flakes begin to flutter in front of my eyes.

"Colin?" I hold out my hand, looking at the little snowflake as it lands and melts in my palm.

He smiles and pulls me close. "I'd do anything for you." He kisses my cheek and whispers in my ear, "I'd make the sun, moon, and stars realign if you asked me."

"You made it snow?" Tears spring into my eyes yet again.

He nods. "I remembered you saying how your favorite book as a little girl was about princesses dancing in the snow. Every little girl wants to be a princess on their wedding day, and I couldn't let you be a princess without any snow." He pulls me close, and I nearly fall apart.

I'm not marrying my brother—a guy would tease me about something like this, not move heaven and earth to make it happen without my even asking. No, I'm marrying my sister. I can't bow out. I have to do this.

He takes my hand and leads me to another group of people, milling, wearing an easy fifty thousand bucks a piece in jewelry alone. Weddings are one of those places where people are happy to bust out the bling and display their wealth.

Colin keeps me moving from one group of people to another, making the same introductions and small talk over and over again. People I've never met before air-kiss my cheek, telling me how wonderful it is that I'm marrying Colin. They go into stories about how they thought this boy would never become a man and are all too happy to meet the woman responsible.

When we meet the old money from Texas, it's more than obvious. Who else would wear ostrich quill boots with a tux? The bolero ties are a giveaway, too. The biggest giveaway, however, is how they greet me with genuine warmth, welcoming me with open arms and comfortable hugs.

I'm a liar. They shouldn't be so kind to me. I didn't change Colin. I didn't make the boy into a man. He still likes men! It's making me sick to stand here, smiling, lying to one person after another.

Colin takes my hand, squeezes it, whispering in my ear, "I love you, Beth. You're doing fine. It's almost over." I squeeze back, secretly hoping a bus hits me on the way home.

I don't belong here. Nothing about tonight is real, even the flowing pale apricot gown I'm wearing isn't me. I can't even remember how Mrs. Frey convinced me to wear it. It's more Jane's style than mine, conservative and feminine, with delicate, scratchy lace. The color makes me look sallow. It matches the way I feel inside—ill.

Even Dad noticed.

When I went to Dad's bedroom to kiss him goodbye, his brow furrowed and he asked if I was happy. What could I say? I am as close to happy as I'll ever get, but he knows something deep down is crying out, begging me not to stuff it in a box and banish it to the back of my brain. I can't listen to that part of me right now.

Loyalty matters.

Family matters.

My word is everything.

I can do this.

Mother chats lightly with Jane and Cameron. She's the happiest I've ever seen her. And Jane, she's so radiant everyone around her can't help but return her megawatt smile. Even Mary looks breathtaking. She's got a gothic princess thing going on in her beautiful, black spider web gown.

As I look around the ballroom, I notice Mateo and his sister standing in the corner. His crisp white shirt complements his dark tanned skin and chiseled jaw, but his usually handsome face is consumed with sadness as his dark eyes follow Colin around the room.

He looks just as miserable as I feel.

After meeting yet another senator and his wife, Colin leads me to the center of the ballroom, where his parents wait with dozens of photographers and reporters.

The portrait photographer Mother hired throws out instructions, moving us to our spots to ensure the photo of our first public kiss "accidentally caught" by photographers is perfect. It's all fake.

I'm like a Barbie doll. Put one hand here, the other there. Turn this way. No, a little to the right. Perfect. On command, I tilt my head, and that's when I see him.

Darcy.

He stands near the entrance of the ballroom with his hands loosely held in front of him. That handsome face is well trained in that familiar mask he always wears to shut the world out—to keep everyone away. When our eyes meet, I think he's going to freeze me out. For a moment it's all ice and steel, but then that façade falls and I can see pain flash behind his eyes.

Today should be a day of celebration. Instead, I'm biting my lip, trying not to let the sob stuck in my chest escape. I can feel it rubbing the bottom of my ribs, carefully lodged in place, brewing silently beneath the surface.

The fake smile I'm wearing is about to crack.

My eyes flick from Darcy to Mateo to Colin. This is wrong. Everyone is miserable, too afraid to be with the person they really love. We're resigned to silently be the good son and the dutiful daughter. I'm not sure I know what that means anymore. Hurting Darcy is the last thing I want, and yet I know walking down the aisle with Colin will shatter him. I saw the desperate longing in his eyes, heard the desire in his voice.

And Mateo, dear God. The man is a sheet of thin ice. His exterior is frosty, but melting quickly. His sister's hand is on his shoulder, as if she's trying to lead him away, but he won't move. He stands there, diligently waiting for his soul mate to confess the truth.

It'll never happen. Colin won't put his family through that. He thinks he's doing what's right. Darcy's gaze holds mine and we seem to have a silent understanding that everything between us, no matter if love is present or not, is over.

I'm over you, Mr. Darcy. Walk up to him and say it. Put him out of his misery so he can move on. He doesn't need to know how I really feel about him, how I adore him. Or that I fell in love with him somewhere along the way. He doesn't need to hear that I wish his face could be the last thing I saw every night and the first thing I see each morning. He shouldn't know the longing I feel for him whenever I hear his name. It's like conjuring a ghost, and for a second, I can breathe again, pretending he's there, getting lost in his remembered embrace.

There's no room for memories, no tears can be shed for lost loves. That part of my life is over. I chose this and I'll die keeping my promise.

Just like Colin will die keeping his secret.

Nausea heats my body and twists the room. It feels like there are fingers around my throat, squeezing.

Colin follows my gaze to Darcy, breaks his pose, and takes me into his arms. "What's wrong, Beth?"

I place my hands on his chest and gaze into his eyes, ignoring the photographers and reporters. Gently, I brush his soft hair off his face. "Nothing. It's just warm in here under all the lights."

"Right, of course. Let's step outside for a moment." Colin puts his hand on the small of my back, and leads me past everyone, past Darcy, completely ignoring Mateo, until we're on the balcony.

A wisp of winter wind sends my curls flying from the nape of my neck. My stylist is going to kill me. I can imagine her burning a hole in the carpet, pacing with a can of hairspray and a comb, ready to attack me as soon as I walk inside.

Colin walks to the edge of the balcony. The city sleeps below, encased in the glow of newly fallen snow. He rubs his hands over his face once, and sounds defeated. "I don't know what to do."

A dozens lights flash as I cross the balcony, rise on my toes, and kiss the tip of his nose. I wish we were alone, but even through the glass, they're there. The press will always be following us—waiting. One day, one of us will mess up. I just hope it's not me. How long can I avoid Darcy? Social circles run small amongst this crowd, and Colin doesn't have plans to reside in Texas. I'll continue to see him.

I'll want him to talk to, for comfort, for laughs, for all those things he said in the arcade. I realize I want also want them, but it's too little, too late.

Colin holds my hand and pulls me to the railing. He drapes one arm over my shoulders, as if we're dreaming about our future together while watching Manhattan disappear in a blanket of snow. He presses his lips together into a thin line, quiet for way too long. It's not like him to be serious, not like this.

"I see the way you look at William Darcy. Is there something going on there?" His voice is stiff with fear, laced with regret.

"Not anymore. I might have had a fling with him a while back, but it never went anywhere." I watch the snowflakes flutter past my nose and repress a shiver.

OVER YOU

Colin takes off his tux jacket and drapes it over my shoulders. Still keeping our backs to the windows, he stares off into the city while he speaks. "Because of me."

"No, it wasn't you. I made that mess myself. It was before I even agreed to marry you—you're clear."

He smirks and glances over at me. "I'll never be clear. I'll always be looking over my shoulder, wondering who's watching."

He laces his fingers through mine and lifts our hands before kissing my fingers. "You'll never forgive me if we go through with this."

"Forgive you for what? Colin, I'm the one who said yes. I could have said, no, suck it up and move on with your life. I didn't. I'm here now. I always will be." I look up into his baby blue eyes and see so much emotion.

"I know. That's why I have to do this." I'm not sure what he's thinking, but Colin presses my hand to his lips a second time, drops it, and walks away.

I follow him inside and snatch his arm. "We're almost done. The finish line is less than a day away. Colin, stop!"

But he doesn't slow. I rush to keep up with him, his jacket slipping off my shoulders as I rush by Darcy. He watches us, but doesn't move.

Colin stops abruptly and turns to me. He clasps my hands between his palms. "That's just it. This is not the finish line. It's the beginning of a long, soul-crushing mistake. I should never have asked you to do this and the fact that you did—I've never had someone show me how much they love me before. I'm eternally indebted to you, no matter what happens next."

I don't like the cryptic language or his dark mood. It's not like him. "Colin, what are you doing?"

"What I should have done a long time ago." I watch as his perfectly pressed white tux shirt makes a beeline across the room. He doesn't stop until he's in front of Mateo. Colin offers a hand and leads the other man onto the dance floor. Mateo has tears in his eyes and can't stop smiling.

Cameras move past me, following him to the ballroom floor, watching something no one dares put words to, until it's impossible to think anything else. Colin pulls Mateo to him, rests his pale hands on Mateo's dark cheeks, and leans in. The kiss is shy, brief, and indisputable.

Flashes go off, blinding me. I turn and notice that some of the photographers are watching me. Lights flash in my face, but I point back to Colin. It's not over.

Colin addresses his horrified parents. "I need to tell you something about me. Love isn't always wrapped pretty in a silk chiffon dress." He presses his lips together and reaches for Mateo's hand. "Sometimes it takes a turn no one saw coming, and the truth of the matter is…"

The room is silent. The orchestra has fallen silent and I swear to God, Mr. Frey's brain is frying in his skull. I can almost hear it. Colin's mother has a softer expression—still horrified, but hiding it as best she can.

Before Colin can say it, she crosses the short distance between them. "I already know. We both do."

The instant she says it, the flashes go off again, some reporters photographing his parents' reaction, the whole room a roar of whispering socialites. Colin holds up a hand, and the room falls silent again, all eyes and cameras trained back on him.

"Dad, I don't care if you accept me for who I am or not. I have my family," he glances over his shoulder at me, "and they love me for who I am. I'll always be your son, but I can't be the fake golden child you want any more, and I won't ruin other people's lives to maintain your idea of me. This is who I am, and, if he'll have me, Mateo is the man I plan to spend my life with."

In the shocked silence that follows, Colin turns and holds out a hand for me. I walk over to him and allow him to kiss my cheek. He whispers, "Sorry for the drama. I promise the rest of the year will be drama-free."

I press the end of his nose and smile. "Don't make promises you can't keep. You know you love the drama."

He grins. "I do. Watch this." Colin turns and walks to Mateo who is shrinking back into the corners.

Colin drops to one knee in front of him and says, "Will you marry me?"

The flood of camera shutters clicking obscures Mateo's answer, but I can tell from their expressions and the excited roar of the guests that Mateo says yes.

I glance back at Mr. Frey who is still staring, shocked, in his son's direction. A campaign consultant pops out of the crowd and whispers something into his ear. Instantly, all the lights switch back on in his head, and he crosses the room to meet Mateo and shake his hand. It may not save his campaign, but it's a start at saving his relationship with his son, and I'm grateful.

I scan the ballroom. Darcy's still standing in the same spot as before, arms folded across his chest.

Our eyes lock for a moment. For the first time in my life, I know exactly what I want.

I want William Darcy tied up with a big red bow.

He takes a hesitant step toward me and stops, questioning. I run across the ballroom toward him, dodging reporters and well-meaning guests as I make my way to him, stopping just short of touching. His hand drifts toward my face, then drops as if he's afraid to touch me.

Now that I'm here, I don't know how to begin. I clear my throat and jump in, "After everything you've done for my father, and for Jane, too, I need to thank you. Dad wouldn't have made it without your intervention."

"You found out." He looks away, embarrassed.

I close the distance between us, gently touching his cheek, turning him to me. "Yes. No more secrets."

He opens his mouth to speak and then closes it quickly. His eyes drift down to the floor. "Secrets like what you were willing to do for your friend, Colin?"

I drop my hands, and shy away. "The entire world probably knows about that by now. We're about to be a YouTube sensation."

Sapphire eyes flick to mine with admiration. "Your ability to find humor in the most difficult of circumstances fascinates me."

"You and me both." I laugh nervously. How do I tell him? What do I say? What if he doesn't love me anymore? I rub my arms, chasing away the shivers spiraling through my body.

He gazes deeply into my eyes, his face raw with emotion. "You must know I..." He takes a nervous breath. "I did it all for you."

"Oh?"

He nods. "My feelings for you haven't changed. If anything, they've only grown stronger in these past weeks." He swallows thickly. "I tried to move on, but I couldn't. I can't get past it. There is no getting over you. I lo—" His voice breaks with emotion. He clears his throat and tries again. "I love you, Elizabeth Bennet."

His brilliant blue eyes gaze into mine, waiting for a response to his declaration. I slide my hands up his chest, resting them over his heart, feeling it beat wildly underneath my fingertips.

A smile spreads across my face and the truth tumbles out. "I didn't know before, but I see it now. I love you. I've loved arguing with you since the day we met, William Darcy."

My hands make their way to his neck, and I pull him to me. He dips his head, and I gently caress his lips with mine. It's a kiss of hope, of promises, of new beginnings.

I've found my fairytale ending.

He leans back and takes my hand. "Our engagement party should move to a more intimate location." He places a hand on the small of my back and begins to guide me out of the ballroom.

My cheeks burn with the innuendo. Coyly, I look back at him. "I agree. Intimate sounds good. Warm blankets, your hot body, and wicked kisses. A celebration just for two."

He kisses my hand and grins. "I planned on flying away from here as soon as possible, so my jet is waiting at Teterboro Airport. The pilots already have it prepped and ready to go."

Surprised, I stop and look up at him. "Really? Do you have Valentine's Day plans?"

"I do now, well, I mean…I hope so." He smirks, holding my hands as he drops to one knee. "Elizabeth Bennet, will you marry me? Will you be my wife forever and always?"

I can't stop smiling. It feels like I'm going to explode with happiness. I summon enough composure to reply, "Why, Mr. Darcy, I thought you'd never ask."

* * *

READY FOR MORE?

Pre-Order STRIPPED 2 Now!

* * *

To ensure you don't miss H.M. Ward's next book, text
HMWARD (one word) to 24587 to receive a text
reminder on release day.

COMING SOON:

MORE FERRO FAMILY BOOKS

JONATHAN FERRO
~STRIPPED~

******

TRYSTAN SCOTT
~BROKEN PROMISES~

******

NICK FERRO
~THE WEDDING CONTRACT~

*****

BRYAN FERRO
~THE PROPOSITION~

*****

SEAN FERRO
~THE ARRANGEMENT~

******

PETER FERRO GRANZ
~DAMAGED~

******

MORE ROMANCE BY
H.M. WARD

SCANDALOUS

SCANDALOUS 2

SECRETS

THE SECRET LIFE OF TRYSTAN SCOTT

DEMON KISSED

CHRISTMAS KISSES

SECOND CHANCES

And more.

To see a full book list, please visit:
www.HMWard.com/#!/BOOKS

CAN'T WAIT FOR
H.M. WARD'S
NEXT STEAMY BOOK?

Let her know by leaving stars and telling her
what you liked about

OVER YOU

in a review!

ABOUT THE AUTHOR
L.G. CASTILLO

Known for her high-intensity New Adult Romance novels, Texas psychologist and professor, L.G. Castillo, writes books that explore the tumultuous and psychological journey of self-discovery and falling in love. Her stories feature dramatic, life-changing events interspersed with a good dose of humor, feisty heroines, and the swoon-worthy men who love them. When she's not writing, L.G. is binging on Netflix or adding up frequent flyer miles for her next vacation. She's been married to her own swoon-worthy hero for over two decades.

READY FOR MORE?
READ **YOUR GRAVITY,** by L.G. CASTILLO, NOW!

You can interact with this bestselling author at:
Twitter: @L_G_Castillo
Facebook: LGCastilloAuthor
Webpage: www.lgcastillo.com/

ABOUT THE AUTHOR
H.M. WARD

New York Times bestselling author HM Ward
continues to reign as the queen of independent
publishing. She has sold over 10 MILLION copies,
placing her among the literary titans. Articles
pertaining to Ward's success have appeared in The
New York Times, USA Today, and Forbes to name a
few. This native New Yorker resides in Texas with her
family, where she enjoys working on her next book.

You can interact with this bestselling author at:
Twitter: @HMWard
Facebook: AuthorHMWard
Webpage: www.hmward.com